DRIVING THE BILLIONAIRE WILD

AMANDA CINELLI

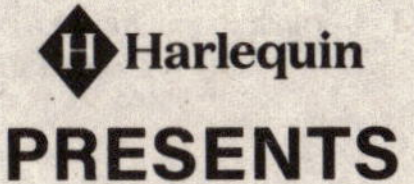

PRESENTS

Recycling programs for this product may not exist in your area.

ISBN-13: 978-1-335-61408-7

Driving the Billionaire Wild

Harlequin Enterprises ULC
22 Adelaide St. West, 41st Floor
Toronto, Ontario M5H 4E3, Canada
www.Harlequin.com

HarperCollins Publishers
Macken House, 39/40 Mayor Street Upper,
Dublin 1, D01 C9W8, Ireland
www.HarperCollins.com

Printed in Lithuania

1 2 3 4 5 6 7 8 9 10 LIT 28 27 26 25

As though she felt his gaze upon her skin, Falco Roux's formidable PR manager looked up, their eyes meeting across the crowded tent that separated them.

Apollo's body had already been thrumming with postrace adrenaline, but quickly that shifted to a familiar simmering heat under his skin. He raised one brow and then winked, and she narrowed her eyes warningly in return. He smirked and tilted his head toward the exit, and Astrid gave her head a firm shake—a signal for him to stay put.

He was well-known for hating the publicity side of being an Elite One driver, regularly sneaking away from interviews early. He'd be lying if he said he didn't enjoy incurring her wrath. Her tart British accent and no-nonsense demeanor had captivated him from the moment she'd walked into their first meeting and laid down the rules. Perhaps because she treated him like every other driver, disregarding his family's reputation and the significant wealth he'd amassed as a businessman in his own right since stepping away from racing for the family team. But this was the usual extent of their interactions; she bossed him around from afar and he tried to ignore how enormously turned on it made him.

The Fast Track Billionaires' Club

Finding passion at the finish line!

In the elite and glamorous world of motorsport racing, it's not just fast cars that get pulses racing… Especially when three billionaires from the exclusive Falco Racing team come face-to-face with the only women who dare challenge them!

Can former Falco driver Grayson ignore his long-buried desire for the forbidden when he's reunited with his best friend's widow?

Find out in Grayson and Izzy's story

The Bump in Their Forbidden Reunion

What will happen when an argument between Tristan, Falco Racing's notorious playboy owner, and the heiress driving for his team goes viral… and forces them into a romance ruse?

Find out in Tristan and Nina's story

Fast-Track Fiancé

What will champion driver Apollo do when he discovers the consequence of his passionate night with a beautiful stranger?

Find out in Apollo and Astrid's story

Driving the Billionaire Wild

All available now!

Amanda Cinelli was born into a large Irish Italian family and raised in the leafy-green suburbs of County Dublin, Ireland. After dabbling in a few different career paths, she finally found her calling as an author upon winning an online writing competition with her first finished novel. With three small daughters at home, she usually spends her days doing school runs, changing diapers and writing romance. She still considers herself unbelievably lucky to be able to call this her day job.

Books by Amanda Cinelli

Harlequin Presents

A Ring to Claim Her Crown

The Avelar Family Scandals

The Vows He Must Keep
Returning to Claim His Heir

The Greeks' Race to the Altar

Stolen in Her Wedding Gown
The Billionaire's Last-Minute Marriage
Pregnant in the Italian's Palazzo

The Fast Track Billionaires' Club

The Bump in Their Forbidden Reunion
Fast-Track Fiancé

Visit the Author Profile page at Harlequin.com for more titles.

CHAPTER ONE

In a lifetime of glamourous global adventures, Apollo Accardi had yet to experience an event more electric than the Italian Elite One Premio. It was even more enjoyable when he'd just won his family's sacred home race in a record-breaking final lap…whilst driving for their most historic rival.

Satisfaction filled his lungs as he strode through the paddock in his iconic maroon Falco Roux racing suit and glared up at the crowd of fans waving a sea of Accardi Autosport white flags. After almost eight years since his mysterious departure from the sport, his mid-season track return last summer had shocked the world. What had started out as an impulsive favour to his friend Tristan Falco had somehow become a chance at redemption he'd never planned to take.

His team mate, Nina Roux, hadn't been the stuck-up heiress he'd been told to expect; in fact she'd been an invaluable ally, even as she'd navigated an unexpected media storm and a personal relationship with Falco, the team owner. Apollo had steered clear of the drama for the most part and had eagerly accepted the opportunity to extend his contract. He'd taken his time, trained hard and spent last winter buried in strategy and analytics.

Now, he was already halfway through his second season with Falco Roux and they had a comfortable lead in the constructors' championship.

And Apollo… Well, he was ready finally to put one particular demon to rest. Winning the elusive Elite One drivers' championship was every driver's goal, one that Apollo had already achieved once, eight years ago, for Accardi Autosport. But this time it would be without his grandfather's influence. This time, it would be on his own terms.

After years of honing his skills as a businessman, Apollo usually knew when a storm was brewing and something didn't feel quite right. It hadn't felt right all day, not since his grandfather had appeared in his private dressing room right before the race and asked if they could speak later—a conversation he'd been avoiding for months.

Perhaps that was the reason for the steady pulse of unease that continued to build within him as he took his seat front and centre in the press tent, shoulder to shoulder with Nina and another driver, who'd each placed second and third respectively. Apollo nodded over to where Falco sat on the sidelines alongside their team principal, Alain Roux, Nina's older brother. The whole team had worked hard this weekend and he was looking forward to a night of celebrations ahead.

But as they all waited…and waited…he felt the tension in the room build. The murmur of voices gradually shifted from impatience to unease as the usually punctually held event was delayed by fifteen minutes, then half an hour, with no word as to what was wrong.

The post-race press conferences were pretty standard

fare; journalists asked pre-cleared questions and drivers offered up answers that were in keeping with their team ethics and the public persona, usually crafted carefully by a collection of professional spinners and gurus. Gurus such as Astrid Lewis, the most coveted publicity expert in the industry. Apollo's eyes scanned the room and found who he was looking for, her full, ruby-red lips pursed as she scanned a phone screen and adjusted the black-rimmed glasses on her pert nose.

As though she felt his gaze upon her skin, Falco Roux's formidable PR manager looked up, their eyes meeting across the crowded tent that separated them. His body had already been thrumming with post-race adrenaline, but quickly that shifted to a familiar simmering heat under his skin. He raised one brow and then winked, and she narrowed her eyes warningly in return. He smirked and tilted his head towards the exit, and she gave her head a firm shake—a signal for him to stay put.

Astrid ruled the entire Falco Roux racing team with an iron fist and, since Apollo's brief attempt at flirtation shortly after he'd joined the team last year, she'd taken to sending her minions to keep his escape antics in check more often than not. He was well known for hating the publicity side of being an Elite One driver, regularly sneaking away from interviews early.

He'd be lying if he said he didn't enjoy incurring her wrath. Her tart British accent and no-nonsense demeanour had captivated him from the moment she'd walked into their first meeting and laid down the rules. Perhaps it was because she treated him like every other driver, disregarding his family's reputation and the significant wealth he'd amassed as a businessman in his own right since stepping away from racing for the family team. But that was the usual extent of their interactions: she bossed him around from afar and he tried to ignore how enormously turned on it made him.

So he was quite surprised when Astrid stood from her seat and crossed the room, coming to a stop by his side at the long interview table.

'Have I broken one of your rules, Ms Lewis?' he teased, his smile dropping slightly when he took in the absence of colour on her usually pink cheeks. She laid one hand on the table and he felt his blood turn to ice, because the utterly unflappable Astrid Lewis was trembling.

'Apollo… I need you to come with me.' Astrid smoothed her other hand down over her black skirt, concern marring her brow. 'I've been told the delay is due to an emergency. There's an ambulance outside the Accardi motor home… it's your grandfather.'

As he tried to make sense of her words—of why they should be told in such a hushed tone, as if she was sorry—phones began to ping across the room. The journalists in the throng followed one another in staring at their screens then immediately glanced up towards Apollo.

'A heart attack? Enzo Accardi?' A young woman in a crisp white Accardi team shirt breathed, then with a sob clapped a hand over her mouth. The exit of the tent opened and the faint flash of blue lights appeared, briefly casting a glow over everyone's faces.

'Is it true? They're saying he didn't make it,' a reporter called out.

Apollo rose from his seat, his chair hitting the wall with a crash. He was hardly aware of his own body before he began to push through the crowd towards the side entrance. Warm summer air filled his lungs before he took off at a sprint as dread filled his gut. It wasn't him; it couldn't be. His grandfather was indestructible.

The closer he got to the Accardi team's headquarters, the blue lights grew stronger. A single ambulance sat outside, the doors open wide. Two paramedics sat on chairs nearby, looking utterly defeated. As he neared them, one stood up, a look of pity on his face as he recognised Apollo. He hardly registered the man speak, the words, 'Sorry,' and 'He's gone,' vaguely seeping into his consciousness.

No. He felt his world slow down to a stop, a lifetime of memories taunting him: his grandfather taking him to the track for the first time to escape his parents' loud screaming matches; his grandfather lifting him onto his shoulders after his first trophy win. When it had felt as if no one else had had any time for him as a child, Nonno had been an ever-present force, criticising him, pushing him, infuriating him, loving him. It was only later, when Apollo was an adult, that things had started going wrong between them.

'Apollo.'

Vibrant green eyes etched with concern moved into his line of sight, pulling him out of his frozen stare. He looked down and saw that she'd followed him, his prickly English rose with her seriousness and calm. She was the opposite of him in every way and yet, when her hands covered his, the warmth of her touch calmed him.

'I'm getting us out of here, okay? Don't move.'

She formed a barrier with her small frame between the crowd and him, something that might have seemed humorous to him any other day. Instead, he remained still, studying how she gestured with one hand to someone in the crowd and tapped furiously on her phone with the other. Her eyes met his, strong and steady, and he clung to their green depths; to the perfect slant of her nose and the arched bow of her lips.

He clung to all that he knew to be steady and true… because, if Enzo Accardi truly was dead, then everything in his life was about to change.

Being a seasoned crisis PR management expert in the most competitive and dramatic league in motorsport, Astrid Lewis had seen her fair share of scandals on and off the track. Her colleagues often joked that she could sway the entire world's media with one stern look and, truthfully, she had never met a reputation or situation that she couldn't fix. But, as she stared at the video that had begun playing on her phone screen, she felt a whisper of self-doubt coil in her stomach.

Rain battered the windows of the hired car as she adjusted the designer spectacles on the bridge of her nose. 'This is…not what I expected when you called in a Code Red, Tristan.'

Tristan Falco's face seemed to become even more serious from where she'd minimised their video call in the corner of her screen. 'Our star driver has just cancelled his contract in the middle of the season. I'd call that a high-priority emergency, Astrid.'

From what she could ascertain from the grainy footage, the clip had been captured some time during the aftermath of yesterday's funeral, at which the entire Accardi family had been in attendance, including Apollo. She cleared her throat, ignoring the now familiar frisson of butterflies in her stomach at the sight of their star driver, stony-faced as he pushed his way through a throng of paparazzi.

The Accardis were practically royalty to their Italian following and their patriarch's death had brought the entire country to a standstill with an outpouring of grief. The biggest names in racing had flocked to the north of Italy over the past few days to pay their respects at a sombre funeral ceremony that Astrid had watched on live stream from her London home.

'One of the Accardi cousins was ranting on social media,' Tristan sighed. 'The man was drunk, openly accusing Apollo of being glad the old man is dead, that their estrangement was what killed his grandfather.'

'That's low, even for *them*.' Astrid shook her head.

'Apollo is refusing to take calls and I was already halfway to Buenos Aires when I was notified about him trying to break his contract. I need you to fix this.'

She pulled up another photo from the funeral, this one of Apollo standing next to his father, Santo Accardi, a world-famous actor. His mother, renowned film director, Leona Hart, had also been in attendance, despite their messy public divorce more than two decades before. Apollo had inherited the best of both of his parents' good looks, with his Grenadian mother's dark complexion and his Italian father's chiselled jawline.

She stared at Apollo's tight expression on her screen a little longer than necessary. Even in grief, the man was far too good-looking; perhaps that was why Astrid always felt uneasy in his presence. The few times she'd found herself alone with him in the past year, she'd found herself tripping over her words. His gaze always seemed to feel a little too intense; it was as if she could feel the heat of it upon her skin. Which was completely ridiculous, of course; she knew that. She'd long considered herself immune to the charms of the wealthy athletes she represented, but something about Apollo had always made her feel….off-balance. So much so that she'd actually taken to avoiding in-person meetings with him, opting instead to send other members of her team.

She was by no means a coward, but she also was not a saint. Apollo was a flirt, and a damned good one at that. She wasn't foolish enough to think that his flirtations were anything more than another passing moment for him, but for her, they lit up something needy and foolish inside her that she'd long thought buried. He was a distraction she could not afford, and yet here she was, pulling up alone outside his palatial Lake Como estate.

With two famous parents and a billion-dollar sports fashion empire of his own, Apollo was the kind of household name that didn't require much PR. The man never seemed to rest.

'The real boss is being called in to clean up this mess, I see.' Nina Roux appeared over Tristan's shoulder. 'I thought you promised your kiddo that you'd take the month of August off?'

Astrid took in the easy familiarity between her boss and their second-seat driver. It was hard to believe it had been only a year since the scandal that had resulted in them falling in love during the last Elite One summer break.

'I am taking it off, once I sort this out.' Astrid frowned, thinking of how disappointed her son Luca had been that morning when she'd said she needed to make just *one more* quick trip for work. He loved his cool young nanny

Jem, but had been eager for quality time with his mummy. 'He wasn't happy, but I've bribed him with unlimited tours of the transport museum when I get back.'

'Six-year-olds are so easy.' Nina laughed, the other woman clearly remembering her own recent experience of the little boy's fascination with museum tours and collections. Nina, being autistic like Luca, had a special connection with him, something Astrid was very grateful for.

'Almost seven now,' she corrected, remembering she still had to decide on a birthday gift for her not-so-baby boy. They'd been to every exhibit in England at least once but the London Transport Museum was his current favourite. Sadness welled within her when she remembered his stony face as she'd explained she had to leave. He was very selective about when he chose to use verbal communication, but boy, could he cut her down with just a look. She would happily take him to the museum every single day to make up for breaking her promise.

'Can you fix this, Astrid?' Tristan asked. 'We can't lose him right now.'

'The guy is just grieving in his own way,' Nina said, a frown marring her dark brow. 'Everyone acts out of character or loses it in a crisis. Except maybe Astrid, of course.'

Astrid pursed her lips in a weak attempt at a smile, trying and failing not to remember the only night *she'd* ever acted out of character—a time when her own inner chaos had led her to lose herself in sensual abandon with a mysterious stranger—and the permanent reminder she'd been gifted from it. No one knew the truth of how she'd come to be a single mother—heavy emphasis on 'single'. Of course, she wouldn't change a thing, but still she looked away as her boss turned to whisper something into his fiancée's ear that made the other woman instantly blush. The easy intimacy made something twist momentarily in Astrid's chest before she quickly pushed it away.

Tristan eyed her with curiosity. 'If you'd rather be with Luca, of course Nina and I can change our travel plans and return.'

Astrid sighed, knowing that Luca would be fine if she worked an extra day to sort this out. She had vast experience in pulling drivers back from poor decision-making in the heat of a crisis. She recalled Apollo's reaction on the day his grandfather had died: how lost he'd looked; how she'd wished she could shield him from the camera flashes and cruel questions.

'I can fix this,' she said finally. 'You pay me because I'm the best at handling temperamental racing drivers. Leave Apollo Accardi to me.'

CHAPTER TWO

ASTRID SLAMMED THE door of the horrendous taxi behind her and hoisted her petite overnight bag onto her shoulder, gripping her briefcase in the other hand. While the flight from London to Milan had been relatively straightforward and pleasant, everything since her arrival had been utter chaos. A baggage handler strike had caused massive queues, with her private chauffeur having a breakdown and no replacement being available for hours, so she'd eventually capitulated and booked a taxi, thinking, how bad could it be?

Pretty bad, it had turned out. The man had had her clinging to the door handle as he'd careened around every back road from the city out to the picturesque little lakeside town where the Accardi family brand had been born, a town that was currently in the peak of the summer tourist season. All of that, only to make it to the gates of the address Tristan had provided to find a crowd of photographers and a trio of bullish security guards preventing her entry. She'd shown her PR credentials, and they'd eventually cleared her entry on their ear pieces, but her taxi was not allowed in, so she'd been forced to haul her small overnight bag and briefcase up the mile-long gravelled drive—in five-inch heels, no less.

Her chest heaved with a mixture of exertion and outrage as she rounded a cherub-filled fountain and looked up at the façade of an impressive lakefront villa that she was pretty sure she had seen before in a movie.

It was no secret that Elite One racing drivers had wealth, but the sprawling Lombardy estate seemed to be on a whole other level of ostentation. She found herself letting out a little, 'Woo,' as a butler opened the arched double front-door and descended the steps to greet her, white gloves and all.

'Come in, quickly,' the elderly man said, his melodic voice completely at odds with the deep scowl that dominated his face.

Astrid frowned as she was hurried inside to a grand hall with marble and gold gilt everywhere she looked. She didn't have much of a chance to take it all in, however, as a trio of beautiful women dressed in black descended the grand staircase at the end of the hall in a fit of giggles. She recognised one of them as a model she had managed for an Elite One clothing campaign a number of years before, and tipped her head in brief greeting. The women's heels clicked along the tiles, smiles fading as they caught sight of her and the butler, who was evidently even less amused by their appearance than he had been at Astrid's.

'*Scusate*, guests may only exit by water taxi.' The butler gestured wildly with a thoroughly Italian hand gesture. 'One moment, *signorina*.'

'Apollo is expecting me,' she lied confidently, adjusting the strap on her briefcase with an air of impatience. 'If you can just point me in his direction.'

The man hesitated a moment, but Astrid raised one delicate brow and waited. To her relief, he sighed and rattled off brief directions before guiding the other women through a set of double doors, leaving her alone.

Either the old man's directions were off or the hallways in the grand villa were moving of their own accord, because Astrid quickly found herself in another identical hall with no clue where she was. The sound of loud music floated from somewhere in the house like a ghostly siren's call. A look inside the first open doorway showed a scene of utter chaos with a small crowd of people apparently sleeping upon floor cushions and sofas, whilst almost every available surface was covered in champagne bottles and glasses.

'Is he hosting a funeral or a bachelor party?' Astrid muttered to herself as she stepped round a trail of clothing and what appeared to be confetti strewn along the next hallway. More evidence of heavy partying emerged through a long glass window that looked out onto a modern indoor pool and cabana area filled with even more bottles of expensive alcohol. One man lay asleep on a lounging chair, completely nude except for a swathe of white *faux* fur around his shoulders.

From a PR point of view, this was an utter disaster for a man who was being accused of celebrating the death of his famous grandfather. Still, not the worst party aftermath she'd been subjected to in her career. This might explain Apollo's impulsive decision to break his contract; wealthy drivers often let loose during breaks in their gruelling training regimes. This industry was a pressure cooker of sorts. But Apollo had been raised in this world, in a powerful family where appearances were everything. He should know better—a harsh truth she planned to inform him of immediately before they got to work cleaning up this mess.

The music grew louder as she reached a new wing of the house and she followed, finding herself on a mezzanine level that looked down upon a second indoor swimming pool. This one was Olympic length and ran alongside a fully fitted, glass-walled commercial gym. A curved staircase led her down to the ground floor of the bright space, the source of the pounding rock music now undeniable.

A man emerged from the far end of the pool and Astrid jumped, realising she was looking at the broad expanse of Apollo Accardi's famously muscular back. Not that she had memorised his body; it was just hard not to recognise him with the rather distinctive tapestry of swirling tattoos that decorated his rich brown skin. The music drowned out any hope of him hearing her, so she was forced to pursue him through a series of rooms filled with high-tech training equipment, her breath heaving in her lungs.

She passed through, noting an expensive electronic simulation racing set-up was paused, the screen showing the new track layout for the next race, one month away in Monaco. So typical of an Elite One driver to throw a raging party in the wake of a family funeral, but still spend the next day training harder than any other athlete.

But all thoughts swiftly left her mind when she entered the next room to find the man himself braced over a large steel bath tub, muscles rippling in the midday light that streamed in from the glass-domed roof above. Mouth dry, Astrid cleared her throat to announce herself and fought not to squirm when dark eyes pinned her in place.

She knew the ice bath he was slowly lowering himself into was to reduce muscle pain after heavy training and competitions. She knew this because racing drivers were her speciality, but Apollo…. She never could figure him out. Even now, with his eyes raking up her body in a slow assessment, she felt her skin prickle with awareness and had to resist the urge to cover her chest…just in case her treacherous breasts gave her away through the secure padding of her bra.

'Astrid.' His husky voice was a low growl as he submerged himself fully into the icy water without so much as a shiver. Still not breaking eye contact, he steeled his jaw. 'If you're here to babysit me some more, I'm afraid you've travelled for nothing.'

'Babysitting is not an option, now you've already made your mess. I'm here to clean it up.' She spoke in a deliberately neutral tone, setting her briefcase and overnight bag down gently on the tiled floor before crossing her arms. 'I understand you are grieving.'

'I'm not grieving. I'm done,' Apollo said calmly, his eyes closed, and head tilted back in a way that put the impossibly thick expanse of his neck on full display. She mentally shook herself, standing up to her full height.

'Your cousins are already trying to use your grandfather's passing to smear your name. Your behaviour is not helping matters.'

The few times she'd met him, he'd usually smiled at her and flirted, but not today. Today, he just seemed exhausted. Grief did that to people, she supposed, and felt a pang of guilt at what she was here to try and make him do. She realised how strange it must have been, going from winning an Elite One Premio to burying the man who had helped forge his career in the space of a few days. Maybe that was what she needed to appeal to: the memory of the man he'd lost, and to ensuring Enzo's name wasn't tarnished. She took a seat on a nearby bench, crossing her legs as demurely as she could manage in her knee-length skirt.

'Look, I know that you and your grandfather had been estranged for a number of years, and I understand his death must have come as a shock.'

'The man thrived on coffee and cigarettes, not to mention he never took a damned day off in fifty years. It was a shock he lived this long.' He paused, meeting her eyes. 'Did I tell you that he called me? The morning of his heart attack. He asked if we could talk. I'd heard he had been in poor health over the past year… Still, I said no. I didn't realise it was this serious.'

Astrid blinked at the emotionless delivery of his words. Brown eyes met hers and for a split second she saw under the facade. This man wasn't just exhausted and grieving.… he was also furious.

'Give me an hour,' she cajoled softly. 'We can talk through the situation over lunch and, if you're still sure of your decision, I'll go.'

'Ever the professional, Ms Lewis,' he growled. 'I don't need or want Falco Roux stepping into my family conflict. As I'm sure you're aware, I'm no longer your concern.'

'Like it or not, your actions have made this my concern. I've had to fly here on my day off so, if you have decided to suddenly give up your chance at winning the driver's championship, then you have plenty of time to get up out of your little bath and help me fix it.'

Apollo closed his eyes, stretching muscular arms up over his head. 'I'm rather busy at present.'

Astrid felt a flare of irritation. 'Busy recovering from a raging party with a gang of models?' She took a step closer. 'You may have a lot more power than most drivers out there, but your contractual obligations to your team remain the same. In this business, every second counts, and I won't leave until you agree to make a statement.'

'You seem upset about the models, Astrid, are you feeling jealous?' A wry ghost of a smile appeared on his lips, one strong hand rising from the water to trace a lazy path along the rim of the steel tub.

The way he'd said her name sent a warm shiver down her spine. As did the unmistakeable flash of hunger in his gaze. She remembered how openly Apollo had flirted with her during those first weeks, and how quickly and primly she had made clear to him her rules about never dating a driver. He'd flashed her his stunning smile and made a point never to press the issue again. But these hungry looks had persisted…

As had a curiosity of her own at how tempted she'd been to allow her tightly knit boundaries to be unravelled by a man like Apollo Accardi. A vision of what that might look like entered her mind: being held and touched in a way she had denied herself for almost eight years. But she knew all too well what happened when she threw caution to the wind and indulged in a little harmless fun. There was a reason why she kept her world so tightly controlled, after all. She pushed away her moment of weakness and reminded herself of the task at hand.

'Apollo, it's my job to stop drivers from ruining their careers, and I'm damned good at it.' She crossed her arms over her chest, putting on her best stern, no-nonsense attitude. 'So it's in your best interests to let me help you. I won't leave until we have agreed upon a course of action.'

'You're wasting your time,' he growled.

'This is important for your team, and—'

'Not my team any more,' he ground out. 'Now, unless you want an eyeful, I'd suggest you leave while I get out of my *little bath*.'

Astrid paused, taking in the hard line of his jaw and feeling a cold foreboding in her stomach. Despite Tristan's insistence that this was an impulsive action, Apollo seemed utterly serious about breaking his contract. She closed her eyes, pinching the bridge of her nose hard. They could have threatened any other driver with sanctions and fines and kept the upper hand. Apollo was not just any driver, though; he was a man with the power and means to pay his way out of any situation.

Before she could process his warning, Apollo was standing up, water sluicing down over his very muscular, very *naked* body. She couldn't help but see every inch of skin he so brazenly put on show, and felt a blush begin immediately in her cheeks as she fought to look away without reacting.

She almost succeeded too, only for something to grab her attention so suddenly that her entire body seemed to freeze colder than the tub he still stood in. The long, raised, curved line was a darker shade of brown than the rest of his skin, and should have been completely innocuous, considering the tattoos that covered most of his upper torso and back. But this….marking was low in his groin, hidden from usual view.

Like a trigger, a memory unlocked in her mind: a masked auction in Venice; an instant attraction with a handsome stranger who'd made her laugh; her nervous excitement at his offer to go upstairs to the penthouse for a drink…until they'd become trapped in the lift together during a power cut caused by a violent storm.

An agreement to keep their masks on, to stay anonymous. Pleasure so intense, she'd felt forever changed.

Her hands had explored his hard muscles in the semi-darkness of the lift. Her fingertips had followed a long, curved line of a scar, and she'd asked how it came to be. He'd given a vague description of a childhood accident with a bow and arrow, and how he'd wanted to have a funny tattoo designed around it, but hadn't got round to it yet—a tattoo of a bow, sending an arrow free….identical to the one that now sat low on Apollo Accardi's groin.

'I told you I was getting out,' Apollo said gruffly as he grabbed a towel to sling across his hips, shielding his skin from her shell-shocked view. Astrid was only half aware of her own movements as she shakily took a step backwards, half-stumbling over her luggage on the floor. Her stomach tightened as her eyes rose up to lock on his face. This wasn't real. It couldn't be. Because if it was…

'Are you okay?' Apollo asked, frowning now. 'You look like you've seen a ghost.'

Perhaps she had. Or perhaps her mind had just finally made the connection with the memory that her body seemed to have recognised instantly the moment this powerfully built, enigmatic man had walked into her meeting room on the day he'd signed his Falco Roux contract last summer, and every damned day ever since. His accent was different, his body covered in tattoos and more muscles that the man she remembered. It *couldn't* be him, and yet…

It was.

Her breathing shallowed and a tremor began in her legs

so suddenly that she feared she might collapse completely. So, she did the only logical thing she could think of when faced with the realisation that the most famous driver in Elite One racing was the father of her six-year-old son.

She grabbed her bags and ran.

CHAPTER THREE

It took a moment for Apollo's brain to catch up with the amount of effort he was expending to keep the physical reaction of his body under control. Being around Astrid Lewis was an exercise in sensual torture at the best of times, but in his current mood… He cursed and stepped quickly out of the ice bath, realising he had behaved badly.

Scooping up a pair of workout shorts from a nearby surface, he ignored the sensation of his still wet and freezing-cold skin as he pushed through the terrace doors into the warm summer air.

She'd barely had a minute of a head start but had made impressive progress across the gravelled courtyard that backed the rear wing of his estate. As he called out her name, he saw the whip of her light brown hair in the breeze as she broke into a run, her heels, a briefcase and a small bag causing her difficulty across the soft lawn in the direction of the lakeside dock.

His butler had spent most of the morning ushering guests from last night's entertainment without the press seeing them. It had been his father's choice to throw a celebration in the wake of Nonno's death. Santo Accardi was used to having full use of Apollo's Lake Como estate, so by the time Apollo had arrived back from a day of meetings in Milan with Enzo's lawyers, and had realised the extent of the festivities taking place in his home, he had been unable to stop things.

Who was he to tell anyone how to grieve? Papa was a free spirit and had been excommunicated and disinherited from the Accardi family before Apollo had ever been born, punished for his refusal to join the family business in favour of his chosen career in film.

Santo's and Apollo's relationship had suffered somewhat when Apollo had accepted his grandfather's invitation to pursue his racing interests seriously. His mother had been busy saving her own career and heartbroken by the divorce. His father had sunk further into his life of casual sex and partying post-divorce, so Enzo had stepped in as his father figure. With every year in which Apollo's talent had become more obvious, Nonno had become more invested in fostering it, and his relationship with his parents had suffered further.

They had reconnected in recent years since Apollo had broken all ties with Accardi Autosport, but a weight in his stomach grew as he remembered he would soon have to tell Santo that Enzo had completely disregarded his only living son's existence in his last will and testament… Santo had been the second-born son, who had grown up in the shadow of his successful racing driver brother. Apollo's Uncle Domenico had passed away during a routine neck operation the year before his parents' divorce, the tragic death leaving his three cousins without a father. It had likely contributed heavily to his own father's out-of-control behaviour and his grandfather's increased interest in Apollo's desire to race, he thought.

But, instead of splitting his estate equally between

his four grandchildren, Enzo had decided to leave sole ownership of Accardi Autosport to Apollo. It was a move that had stunned him to his core and had the potential to launch shockwaves through both Apollo's career and the entirety of Elite One racing. A fact that the old man would have well known, Apollo thought darkly, as he broke into a sprint across the gravelled courtyard in pursuit of the beautiful woman who had intruded upon his intention to brood alone for the entire day.

He finally caught up with her as she stood motionless, watching a water taxi filled with tired party guests move away from the small jetty across Lake Como. The butler stood by her side, apologising as he explained another vessel could be arranged.

'So much for you refusing to leave my property,' Apollo said, his body bracing against the cool breeze coming off the lake onto his naked chest. He didn't miss the way Astrid's eyes took in said naked chest for a split second before she quickly looked away again, the same panicked look in her eyes that he had seen in his gym.

Something about her entire reaction was off. The woman he had worked with for the past year would not have been so easily cowed by something so ridiculous as a nude man. She was legendary in the industry, with stories of her skill at wrangling out of scandals even the most dramatic of drivers. Many teams had tried to sway her to their side, coveting this force of nature whose gift it was to meld narratives and harness public opinion for those who needed it.

But he knew there was nothing she could do to spin this as anything other than a PR disaster for Falco Roux. He couldn't continue to drive for Falco Roux and own a rival team at the same time. But he couldn't prove that he hadn't known about inheriting the family team he'd walked away from almost eight years ago. The only person who could do that was dead.

'I'm sorry for my actions back there; there is no excuse for it, so I won't make one.'

'It's fine,' she said quietly, still studiously avoiding his gaze as she pulled out her phone and began tapping on the screen.

'Come back inside, Astrid. You can continue to berate me for my unreasonable behaviour and I'll be sure not to flash you again.' She didn't make a move to follow him. Resisting the urge to glower, he crossed his arms over his chest. 'You said that you don't give up. Have you suddenly decided I'm a lost cause, then?'

She shook her head, gulping in a breath as though she couldn't quite get enough air into her lungs. Was she having a panic attack? Had the sight of his naked form rattled her so much that it had escalated her into a state of fear? The realisation that he knew nothing about this woman or her history and that he might've done something unintentionally traumatic was a stark one, tightening his own chest.

'I feel the need to affirm that you are safe here, Astrid. With me. I didn't mean anything by my actions other than perhaps to make you leave me alone.'

'I know you didn't. This isn't about that,' she said, a tremor in her voice as she let out a strange laugh under her breath before shaking her head. 'This was the last thing that I expected when I agreed to travel all the way here today.'

'But you did come here and I've been a terrible host. Let's go back inside and you can school me over lunch.'

She waited only a moment before following him, and he felt the bands around his chest loosen slightly once he'd got her back inside the warmth of his home and instructed his butler to take her to a private sitting room to give her some space until lunch was served. He took the stairs two at a time up to his own bedroom, feeling a renewed thrum of adrenaline heating his body at the prospect of wining and dining his guest.

He had initially been surprised by the powerful attraction he felt for the English PR expert, considering how far she was from his usual type. Sure, she was beautiful, and had a curvaceous body that had immediately set his mind to sin the moment he'd first seen her. Usually, he preferred his entanglements to be with women who enjoyed the same fast-paced lifestyle that he did, with adventure and thrills being his main point of focus whenever he wasn't training and competing.

Astrid, on the other hand, seemed to him to be a complete workaholic, with very little time for spontaneity or mischief in her jam-packed schedule. She had a no-nonsense attitude, and had made it very clear from the get-go that she never got involved romantically with her drivers. She was sharp-tongued, uptight and polished and for some reason those details had only solidified his attraction to her even more, making him wonder in how many ways he could unwind the knots in her perfectly straight spine.

Perhaps her appearance here today was fate, he mused as he stepped into the bathroom and undressed, surveying the swathe of tattoos he'd accumulated over the past few years once he'd been away from his grandfather's strict influence and obsession with image. He hardened at the memory of how Astrid had stared at his body when he'd stood up from the ice bath. She'd looked at him with so much intensity…as though seeing him for the first time.

Could it be that his prim and proper PR lady was finally ready to admit she wasn't immune to his charms after all? A smile formed on his lips as he stepped into the large waterfall-shower stall and blasted the water on hot.

Perhaps the one perk that might have come from this inheritance fiasco was that, as of today, he was no longer one of Astrid Lewis's drivers. She no longer had that excuse as to why she denied the obvious attraction between them. She was now free to do as she wished…and that possibility had him speeding up as he went through the motions of getting dressed.

The dining room of Apollo's home was just as lavish as the rest of the mansion she'd seen so far. With a wall of windows providing stunning views of the lake, the marble tiled space was bright and simple with accents of colour in the modern paintings that lined the other three walls. She sat quietly at the end of a grand dining table where an elaborate feast had been set out that would easily have fed ten people. Although, perhaps the excess was necessary, she thought ruefully as she watched Apollo devour two helpings of the tender Tuscan baked chicken and rosemary potatoes, along with an entire side plate filled with steamed greens.

She, on the other hand, merely picked at her food, despite it being utterly delicious. His chef, a kind-faced older Italian woman, had seemed delighted by Astrid's sudden appearance and had already come out once to see if the food was to her liking before retreating back to the kitchen area. Guilty at her lack of appetite, Astrid forced herself to take another large mouthful of chicken and felt Apollo's eyes follow the movement.

'Eat up; we kept the dungeons underneath the estate for a reason.' He smirked, reaching across her to grab the jug of water. At Astrid's shocked look, he laughed low and huskily in his throat. 'Chef Linnea won't be offended if you're not hungry, so relax.'

'The food is wonderful… I'm just out of sorts today.' She pushed away her plate and focused on sipping the iced lemonade she'd selected from the drinks trolley. Part of her wished she'd selected something a little stronger. Her insides still hadn't quite recovered from that strange moment of déjà vu in the gym and, as Apollo began casually to discuss the gym renovations he'd had installed in the house, she struggled to focus. She knew he was making small talk for her benefit. He was smoothing the way before getting into the difficult subject of how to rectify the PR situation that she had been sent here to tackle.

But she had an entirely different problem now, one that involved a certain scar and its connection to a night she had long ago decided to forget.

Perhaps…it wasn't him.

Perhaps the stress of her journey to Italy had induced some kind of emotional hysteria and she'd been pulled back into the memory of the one night in her entire life in which she had allowed herself to lose control completely. Of course, she had been in Italy many times since that fateful stormy night in Venice, but maybe her intuition was off. Maybe it was a coincidence. Maybe…

Memories of that night washed over her: memories

of strong hands soothing the anxiety from her shoulders as they spoke softly in the dim light of the broken-down lift. She'd been twenty-one, and it had been a few months after the break-up with her first boyfriend, Ian, and their disastrous, short-lived engagement. She'd craved freedom and something that was all of her own choosing instead of her parents'. At some point, soft conversation with her masked stranger had turned into frantic kissing, undressing and pleasure such as she'd never experienced in her only other sexual relationship, which had been mediocre in comparison. She'd walked away, confident in her anonymity, considering the only reason she'd been in Italy was as part of a random challenge in her very first Elite One internship to try to win a golden helmet statue in a secret auction.

That one night had changed the course of her life in every way possible. First, she'd failed to get the helmet and had wound up trapped for an hour in a dark lift with a stranger. They'd used protection, but somehow it must have failed, as against all odds she'd discovered she was pregnant. She'd tried to find her mystery lover by enquiring from the same Venetian hotel, but she'd fallen foul of guest confidentiality clauses.

She'd been sheltered and naïve, and had gone from being the good and dutiful daughter of fiercely traditional parents to being a complete pariah. Perhaps that was why she'd decided to hide her pregnancy for much longer than she should have in her brand-new job for one of the mid-league racing teams. One of their drivers, Grayson, had discovered her secret and become an unlikely friend and ally, demanding she be given a permanent contract as part of his personal media team with full maternity pay, and taking her up the ranks with him as his fame had grown and other teams had vied for his attentions.

She'd moved with him to Falco Roux just as their team's PR operation was crumbling. She'd taken the helm, becoming their youngest head of PR by the time Luca was two. She'd maintained a dignified silence on the circumstances of Luca's conception, only ever saying that the father was not in the picture. But she refused to regret it; that one scandalous experience that had given her the greatest gift she'd never known she needed.

She inhaled a deep breath, doubt flooding her mind even as the details glared at her. This could all be a wild coincidence, right? Surely she should try to confirm her suspicions and find out if Apollo had been there that night in Venice? Then, only then, would she try to tell him the reason why she'd nearly jumped out of her skin at the sight of that oddly distinctive scar, enhanced by a clever tattoo.

Would he even believe her?

As though he sensed her inner turmoil, Apollo stood and suggested that they move their drinks to his private study so that the staff could tidy up. The summer sun was high in the sky, a light breeze making small waves glitter beautifully across the lake. She followed along the narrow corridor, feeling as if she were in a dream...or perhaps a nightmare would be more accurate. This man was her assignment, for goodness' sake. Her boss had all but told her that the company's reputation hung upon her convincing Apollo to stay with the team and release a statement squashing the rumours.

If she questioned him about a random encounter, and if she was wrong about it having been him, she'd be humiliated. But she couldn't even begin to think about how it might affect Luca's and her future if she was right. She prized her simple life with her son, their home in London and her career. They were thriving in their new routine and everything seemed to have fallen into place.

Apollo's study was an impressive space, with a slightly darker colour scheme than the rest of the house. One side of the room was dedicated to a large wooden desk and a wall of books and filing cabinets, while the other half of the room seemed to be a meeting space of sorts with sumptuous sofas and a monitor with a sleek video-conferencing set-up in the wall.

She remembered seeing this room in the background during one of their press briefings, as she had studiously tried to avoid staring at the small square on her laptop where his attention had been intensely focused upon her. She had always been so keenly aware of him. Most drivers squirmed during meetings, bored by the business side of the sport they loved, but Apollo was a businessman at heart, as evidenced by the large sportswear brand he had been steadily building during his absence from the sport.

An absence, she suddenly realised, which had begun the same week she'd been in Venice for the auction. He'd walked away from his grandfather's team after a heated argument—over what, nobody knew—and had never returned. Her stomach tightened even more.

At the sound of her name, Astrid's attention snapped back to the present and she saw that Apollo had taken a seat on the sofa and was beckoning her to join him. Nervous energy hummed through her veins as she took a seat on the opposite end from where he sprawled, his dark eyes surveying her with keen interest.

'Is this your only home in Italy?' she asked, sliding out

her tablet from her briefcase and blinking at the image of her son she kept as her screensaver. Gulping, she tapped open the crisis management plan she'd studiously compiled on the flight over and tried to calm her thundering heartbeat. Crisis management indeed; there was no handy list or bullet point plan to navigate how to find out if her work crush was actually the anonymous, scorching-hot encounter that had resulted in her becoming a single mother.

'I have many properties, but none I'd call home,' Apollo replied lazily, one arm extended across the back of the sofa towards her. 'This was the first estate I purchased in Italy. My father lives here most of the year. I do, however, keep my collections here.'

He gestured to a wall behind them, one she must have walked straight past on her way in. The ornate glass shelves formed a modern art installation all by itself, but along them at stylish intervals sat trophies and statuettes, a mixture of his own achievements and art works. And in the very centre…

Astrid choked on the sip of water she'd just taken, tears filling her eyes as she caught her breath. 'The…the golden helmet. You have it.'

He frowned. 'Yes. I won it a long time ago…at a masked auction—'

'In Venice,' she finished for him.

An odd look darkened his features. 'How could you possibly know that?'

Astrid stood up, her tablet falling from her shaking hands. Strong fingers caught it just before it hit the floor, and Apollo's eyes searched hers with confusion. She opened her mouth to speak, to say *something*, but no sound escaped. It was utterly absurd. It was against all reason and logic.

The reality was, the evidence could continue to mount and she would still struggle to comprehend how on earth this had come to be—how she had searched high and low for a stranger who had turned out to be one of the most famous drivers in the very industry she specialised in. Their paths had likely crossed countless times in the years since they'd parted, in the years she'd tried to find him…

The cruelty of it was a strange ache in her chest as she heard his steps crossing the room behind her, his voice warm and husky as he called her name once, then again. She turned, taking in the look on his face and realising he must have asked a question that she had missed.

'I'm beginning to think I need to call a doctor,' he said sternly, the back of one hand lightly touching her forehead. She flinched, taking a step back as though burned.

'I was in Venice too,' she said quietly.

'I would imagine so; working in Elite One, you've been to every major city in the world.'

'I've been to *that* particular auction in Venice.' She forced the words out of her mouth, turning so that their bodies faced one another. 'Almost eight years ago. There was a thunderstorm, the entire city and airports suffered a blackout and the high winds kept rescue busy until morning.'

'Astrid.' Her name was a rough whisper on his lips. His eyes widened with disbelief, his mouth hardening into a line as he simply stared. She felt naked under his gaze, her throat dry as she tried to form the words that rushed to escape her lips. How did she even begin to tell him, to explain?

'I met a stranger at the bar, and we wore masks as part of the auction. He invited me up to his penthouse suite for a drink, in his p-private lift.' She felt her voice shake, but she forced herself to meet his dark gaze. 'We got trapped in the lift for a while. We agreed to keep our identities anonymous, but I think…no, I *know*…that stranger was you.'

CHAPTER FOUR

APOLLO STARED AT the beautiful woman in front of him and wondered how on earth he hadn't seen it before now. That evening, before the blackout, the woman's face had been obscured by an elaborate Venetian mask—as had his own. But he'd noticed her from the moment she'd entered the room.

She'd made him nervous, despite his façade of bravado as he'd pursued her. It hadn't been his smoothest attempt at seduction, but he remembered every moment they'd spent together, just as he remembered how she'd made him promise not to follow her when she walked away.

'Let's leave the magic here,' she'd whispered softly in the darkness as they'd heard the rescue crew arrive outside the lift. 'My life is complicated at the moment.'

In the present, a low laugh of disbelief escaped his lips. 'This is…surreal.'

She shook her head, meeting his gaze for only a split second before moving away again. 'You have no idea.'

'You changed your hair,' he heard himself say, his own voice sounding rougher than he'd intended as he thought of the dark-blonde curls and crisp British accent that he'd so often fantasised about since that night. Self-consciously, she smoothed her hand over her sleek, brown, shoulder-length cut and he mentally cursed.

'This is my natural colour. But, yes, I've changed in a lot of ways.'

In a telling move, she smoothed her hands along the skirt that clung to her hips, hips that were definitely fuller since that night, but had not proved to be an inch less tempting for him and the roaring attraction he'd been holding at bay over the past year. *Dio,* an entire year and she'd been right here in front of him, hiding in plain sight.

'You are even more beautiful than I remember.'

Her breath caught. 'You never even saw my face.'

Apollo fought the urge to grab her hand, to force her to look into his eyes. This woman and their encounter together in the lift had haunted him, branded him. He'd fought himself for months, cursed himself for not tracking her down immediately. By the time he'd snapped and decided to find her, there had been no trail to follow, no clues as to her identity or whereabouts. To think, Astrid Lewis, PR guru and thorn in his side, was the mystery woman who had broken him apart in the dark and made him feel more alive than he could ever remember feeling.

During that first meeting they'd had last year, his body had reacted instantly to her polished accent and he'd been annoyed, thinking perhaps that he'd developed a slight kink for prim English beauties. But perhaps his body had known it was her, even if his mind hadn't made the connection. He'd felt the same pull towards her, the same primal reaction he'd had to that masked beauty on that long-ago night.

'You didn't see my face that night either, Astrid.' He

took a step closer. 'But still, you told me it was the closest you'd ever felt to another person. Then you simply walked away, gone without a trace. Was it all a lie?'

'No, it wasn't. But it wasn't about you. Things were…'

'Complicated,' he finished for her. His jaw ached with how tightly he gritted his teeth, remembering all the scenarios he'd imagined that could be her *complication*, none of which painted her in a positive light. The need to know burned in him, almost as brightly as the need to pull her into his arms and find out if she tasted just as good as his memory insisted she would. 'I'd like to know why you ran from me. What were you hiding?'

'I've not been hiding anything.' She turned to face him, a stricken expression on her face. Her chest heaved against the simple white silk shirt she wore. 'I searched for you…after. I tried to find you, Apollo. I tried my best.'

She'd searched for him? Apollo felt a sudden rush of possession, knowing she hadn't walked away as easily as he'd assumed. Fate had brought her back to him and, this time, he wouldn't let her walk away without a fight.

'What would have happened if you'd found me?' he asked, noting the thrum of her pulse under his fingertips. His own heart beat just as fast, quickening when she looked up at him with pupils blown wide with desire. 'Or did you think that far ahead? Did you wonder how different it might have been?'

She narrowed her eyes, not answering his cajoling questions, but not denying them either.

'I know what would have happened, *bellezza*. You would have come to me and apologised for rushing off, and I would have made love to you all over again until we'd both had our fill. Only then would I have let you out of my sight. Instead, you've haunted me.'

She bit down on her lower lip and instantly he felt his body harden. He imagined claiming those lips with his teeth, soothing the sting with his tongue. The memory of her mouth, of her taste…it would pale in comparison to having her in his arms once again, in his bed. They wouldn't leave it for days, if he had his way.

He allowed her a moment of retreat, seeing the wild look in her eyes. She was still here for Falco Roux as a professional, after all. She would be conflicted about pursuing this any further, given the prim and proper rule-follower that she was. He scoured his mind for all the things he knew about Astrid Lewis. She and her young son lived in London. She kept her home life very private, and race travel time to a minimum, since her son had started school there in recent times. She was a single mother…at least, he had been told she was single now. Had the same been true that night? Had her disappearing act been a necessity, due to a boyfriend or husband waiting for her? The thought sent a bolt of anger through him. He had never been able to abide infidelity, after his father's had torn their family apart.

But, before he could ask that question, a knock at the door interrupted him, announcing the arrival of a helicopter to take him to his afternoon appointment.

'What appointment?' he ground out, half to himself, his mind still clouded with desire.

'It's the mentoring session for Falco Roux at the Milan racing track,' Astrid said softly, her gaze imploring. 'You know how hard those kids have worked, how big a deal this is for them.'

He pinched the bridge of his nose, knowing she was right. It had been the last item on his calendar planned for this week, before his grandfather's death had changed everything. He never missed mentorship events; he knew how vital his presence was to the young teenagers who had earned spots on the programme. Torn between duty and desire, he met Astrid's tentative gaze.

'If there wasn't a group of hot-headed teenage drivers relying on me, there is no way we'd be leaving this room without resolving this. How do I know you'll still be here when I return?'

'I'll go with you,' she said quickly, her fingers flying on her tablet as she took a few paces away from him. 'Some coverage on socials will give us time to figure out your contract issue.'

He could practically see her erecting the walls around herself brick by brick, trying to shut down the frantic heat that had bloomed between them only moments before. As if that was even a possibility, now that he knew who she was.

'You think just because we will be on the race track that I will forget?' Apollo felt some satisfaction as she visibly inhaled a gasp before trying to hide her reaction.

She bit her lower lip again. 'I won't run away. We still need to talk, and I plan to do just that once we calm the media storm. Then I'll tell you everything.'

'Will you?' he asked. 'I think you can see why I might be a little unsure of that. I'll give you this afternoon to resolve the relevant...*professional* details. Then, once that's off your mind, we'll return to our previous discussion. *Si?*'

She waited a beat before nodding once in agreement,

a pretty blush high on her cheekbones. He found himself unable to look away for a moment, his eyes greedy for every detail of her he'd not seen before. He hadn't been lying; he would give her today to calm the PR mess he'd created. He owed the team that much.

But one thing was certain—now that he'd had another taste of his mystery woman, he had to have her in his bed again. Maybe even for the whole summer break, to rid himself of the spell she still held over him. He would have to be tactful, but he would convince her of the same truth. Until then, she wasn't going to leave his sight.

The helicopter flight from Lake Como to the race track was quick but stunning, with the clear sky providing the perfect backdrop for views across the lake region and rural fields. Barely half an hour passed before the more built-up rooftops of Milan came into view, yet still, butterflies churned in Astrid's stomach every time she looked up to find Apollo's brooding brown eyes upon her. He'd been unusually quiet throughout their journey, a fact she'd appreciated as her mind wrestled with the events of the past few hours.

She still couldn't quite believe she'd found the man she'd slept with once and thought of for almost eight years. She'd imagined this day so many times in her mind. She'd imagined finding Luca's father and introducing them; she'd even imagined a kind of fairy-tale happy ending, like she'd seen in romantic comedies. She had a feeling that this…would not be so simple.

Part of her was terrified at the prospect of how the rest of their discussion would go, but the fact remained he was her son's father and Apollo had a right to know, even if his wealth and status was more than a little intimidating. Even if public knowledge about her child's paternity would have the potential to ruin her career. She *would* tell him, once she'd got up the nerve and figured out how to get the words out.

The world-famous Elite One racing track in Milan was, unsurprisingly, named the Accardi Autodrome, and was located just outside the city in the rolling Lombardy hills. She'd been here countless times in her career, first as a young recruit, proving her worth, then waddling around pregnant or carting a wild toddler. That chaotic time had wound down over recent years as she'd transitioned into more senior leadership roles and left the majority of nonessential travel to her team.

The venue staff whom she knew from the previous racing weekend greeted them cheerfully as she and Apollo disembarked from the sleek silver chopper and made their way to the track.

She tried to calm her nerves as she walked alongside him, but found her heartbeat just wouldn't behave. In the space of one morning she'd seen this world-famous racing driver naked, she'd had a life-changing realisation then she'd confessed they had once slept together. Her mind spun; everything seeming almost dream-like as she fought to figure out how on earth she should reveal the rest of the things she'd discovered today. Because she would tell him about Luca; she had to. She had never planned to keep her son's identity from his father and, now that circumstance had given her that chance, she would take it.

She could only hope that Apollo would accept the news.

Would he even want to be part of her son's life? He was

a busy man with a very demanding career; she couldn't imagine him dropping everything to come and attend a morning show and tell. Would he be accepting? Her son's autism diagnosis had been a welcome explanation for his differences, but she'd be lying if she said she hadn't found it overwhelming to process at the start. They'd found an easy rhythm in London with some great teachers and strong routines these past couple of years. Now, the thought of bringing what would essentially be a stranger into his life filled her with worry.

Nerves coiled low in her belly as she took a seat in the viewing area, watching as Apollo appeared moments later on the track below. He had changed into one of his Falco Roux racing suits, a sleek maroon jumpsuit emblazoned with his name and racing number along with various sponsors' logos. He held a helmet in his hands, one of many she knew he had designed specially for every race he'd taken part in. This one was jet-black, with white chevrons at the back.

The small crowd of teenagers in plain driving suits of varying colours quietened when Apollo approached them, their faces awash with nervous excitement as they were greeted by one of the world's most celebrated racing drivers. She couldn't hear what he said as he addressed them, but she knew it would be a balance of charm and encouragement. She'd seen clips of him at events in the past, and as far as PR training went he was a dream. Or at least, he had been...until whatever had got into him this week. He was a consummate professional who had never been part of any scandals, other than the usual on-track drama. His rivalry with Grayson Koh, one of her dearest friends, had been legendary, with the two almost coming to blows many times throughout their careers.

Apollo had been a legend himself, before his sudden unexplained departure from the sport. He'd come third place in his first ever Elite One Premio at the age of eighteen, racing for his family's iconic team, tirelessly working year upon year until finally bringing them to victory in the drivers' championship. Rumours at the time had been that Apollo's fraught relationship with his controlling grandfather and airtight contracts had forced him out of Elite One and into the other leagues of motor racing, where he'd made a name for himself.

As Astrid watched some of the Accardi mechanics join the crowd, with smiles and claps on Apollo's back, she wondered if it had been hard for him to leave.

Shaking off her thoughts, she busied herself with greeting the photographer she'd hired for the afternoon and outlining her plan. Usually, she would have her team with her for official photoshoots or events, but with the league on a one-month summer break she had cleared everyone to work from home. Just as she had planned to do herself, she thought with a groan, as she set up her work station on a bench at the edge of the track.

The next hour passed as she oversaw shots of Apollo's one-to-one mentoring of the teen drivers, instructing the photographer to keep close and focus on building the story she wanted to curate.

She sneakily took some candid shots on her own phone to upload to their team social story when everyone gathered in the garage, just short clips of the group driving around the track, and the serious look on Apollo's face as he slid into the gleaming Falco Roux racing car they'd had transported from Monaco for the day.

He switched easily from English to Italian, with some French thrown in for good measure. Drivers in Elite One tended to speak multiple languages; it was part of the job. On the night they'd first met, had she not noted his distinctively deep baritone? His accent had seemed more typically Italian then—probably because he'd been in his home country, she realised now—but usually it held distinctive inflections from both his parents' cultures, beneath the polished neutral tone he adopted for public speaking.

She quietly watched him behaving in 'racing star' mode but occasionally his eyes slid to where she stood, as though he ensured she was still there. She wasn't sure whether to feel threatened or excited by that knowledge, but she hadn't lied—she wouldn't leave, not until she'd told him the full truth, no matter how much that terrified her.

The big finale of the afternoon mentoring session was a short qualifying race between Apollo and the six academy drivers. Working in Elite One, the actual racing had always just been a background part of her job, one of the few parts that she *didn't* have to worry about and could happily leave to the professionals. But, as she waved the drivers off one by one, she felt…different.

She found herself tensing up as she watched Apollo's car line up on the grid. He'd taken the very last spot behind the other drivers, likely to give them a head start, but once the lights went out and the racing was in full throttle it didn't take him very long to pass them all. Did these cars always need to be driven so fast? Craning her neck, she stood and watched the progress of the drivers as they practically took to the air along the long straight and disappeared from view.

'One would think he'd go easy on them,' a feminine voice drawled from the opposite end of the pit wall.

Astrid turned, instantly recognising one of Apollo's cousins, the PR manager for Accardi Autosport. Allegra Accardi moved with an almost regal grace, her designer suit and perfect blonde chignon seeming to sparkle in the light as she closed the distance between them and leaned in to place the customary Italian greeting upon both of Astrid's cheeks.

'I'm very sorry for your loss,' Astrid said, standing from her seat and trying not to crane her neck to see the view of the racing on the camera monitors behind her. The pit crew and engineers around them had gone suddenly quiet, everyone watching their exchange.

'Grazie.' Allegra smiled, but her dark eyes narrowed in a way that immediately set off alarm bells in Astrid's subconscious.

'Death seems to only encourage the competition in this family.' Allegra's attention wandered briefly to the screen where Apollo still dominated the track. 'Come, let's find somewhere a little more private, shall we? I believe we have *lots* to discuss.'

Apollo felt the tension coming off Astrid's body in waves as he entered the executive suite and both women turned to face him. His cousin stood near the windows, a smirk on her lips as Astrid remained seated with her arms folded tightly across her chest.

'Apollo, I was just filling your PR manager in on

Nonno's last wishes. It seems you forgot to mention that you've just inherited an entire racing team.' Allegra frowned in *faux* concern.

Astrid's eyes met his with a subtle nod, a signal to him not to engage further. A short man with a thin moustache entered the room behind him, announcing that Allegra's presence was needed at a meeting with the Elite One Academy team.

'I'll be right there,' she said with an easy smile. 'Astrid, it was lovely chatting again after so long. It seems not long ago you were waddling around the tracks trying to hide that giant baby bump. The child must be what… six, now?'

'He'll be seven in a couple of weeks.'

She turned her attention to Apollo. 'Time is a thief, as they say.'

He frowned at the unspoken hostility in his cousin's gaze as she bid them both goodbye and strode from the room without further comment. He hadn't expected Allegra to be bold enough to confront him in public, after she'd remained firmly outside the argument with her brothers after the funeral, when they'd discovered he was set to inherit the team. But it appeared she'd just been waiting for her moment. Her comment about time dragged against something in the back of his mind, as had her jab about Astrid. He had never met her son, and had assumed the child was much younger than Allegra had suggested. The knowledge that she'd been with the father of her child so soon after their encounter, or possibly even at the same time, made his stomach tighten with something dark and sharp-edged.

'Did you plan to tell me about the inheritance?' Astrid fumed, green eyes sparking.

'Did you plan to tell me that you weren't single on the night we met?'

'What?' She shook her head, confusion marring her brow. 'Of course I was single. I don't see how that's important right now. Not when you've inherited a whole damn rival team.'

It was important to him, apparently—very important, judging from how the bands in his chest loosened instantly at her honest reaction. Something else still niggled at him, but he'd figure it out later. For now, he had a very agitated Englishwoman to appease.

'I flew all the way here, derailed all of my plans, because Falco Roux takes care of their own. I thought this sudden decision about wanting to break your contract was due to *grief.* But, according to your cousin, you've hidden a crucial fact from the press and you've simply been biding your time as you plot to jump ship to our biggest competitor.'

'Are you asking me if I'm the traitor my cousin implied I am, Astrid?' He stepped closer, bridging the distance between them with two strides. 'Because I thought it was your job to know your drivers better than they know themselves.'

'I can't make an accurate judgement without all the facts.'

'If I had wanted to take over Accardi Autosport, I would have just stayed as their lead driver, pretty much guaranteeing my grandfather would leave it to me.' He waited, watching realisation flare in Astrid's eyes. 'But I chose to walk away. And now, in a last attempt to control my career, he's left me a team that I've never wanted to own.'

'You may not have asked for it, but it's happened and it's—'

'A big fucking problem for me and for Fal. Yes, I know; he knew that too. You understand now why I've refused to speak to the press until I figure out how to proceed?'

An assistant popped her head in, interrupting them and announcing that their helicopter pilot awaited their departure.

'Give us one moment,' Apollo said, but the woman didn't budge, instead explaining that their flight needed to leave immediately or risk being grounded due to high winds. He felt his own frustration peak, his body torn between needing Astrid to understand where his head was at as a driver, and his need to pursue her and get closure on that night in Venice.

Without consulting him, Astrid picked up her briefcase and strode past him.

Silence fell between them as he allowed Astrid space to stew and make her plans, her fingers tapping wildly on her tablet as the helicopter flew them through the rapidly darkening evening sky. The winds were strong, but she was completely engrossed in her work, so engrossed that she hadn't noticed they'd been flying for a lot longer than planned and in the opposite direction from where they'd originally come.

'You could have come to Falco Roux with this sooner. To me.' Her voice finally sounded through the head sets they both wore. She was still staring down at her screen, legs crossed and mouth pursed. 'We need to speak with

Tristan and Alain; set up meetings with the Elite One stewards.'

'This hasn't been a selfish choice, or an easy one. I'm painfully aware of the consequences that breaking my contract mid-season is going to have on Falco Roux. Do you think I want to let Tristan, Nina and Alain down? I have my own team of lawyers who have been investigating the various options and consequences, should I accept the terms of my grandfather's will.'

'You haven't accepted the terms yet?' Her eyes brightened. 'That's great, then…we need to get ahead of this once we get back to your estate.'

He fought the urge to smirk. 'Didn't I say? We're not going back to Lake Como.'

As the view of the glittering waters and historic buildings of their destination became apparent, Astrid's eyes flew to his.

Was it cruel of him to bring her back to the scene of the crime, as such? Perhaps, but there was no way he was going to take her back to his estate with the press surrounding it, not when an extra twenty-minute journey could bring them here instead. She would be intent on fixing his dilemma, of course, and truthfully he liked watching how her brain worked. But, on a more selfish note, he wanted her *here*. He didn't plan to let this opportunity go to waste. Not when she had already made it abundantly clear that she had regretted walking away from him that night without having revealed their identities.

'Welcome back to Venice, Astrid.'

CHAPTER FIVE

A CONCIERGE MET them on the roof of the exclusive Venetian island resort with a team of staff to take their bags and accompany them across the lamplit rooftop garden path. Heavy wind blew at her hair and skirt as she looked out across Venice's famous cityscape and wondered at how on earth she'd ended up back here. This infuriating man was fast wearing out her control and, after the series of revelations she'd endured in the past few hours, she felt a migraine threaten behind her temples.

Apollo took her by the elbow as they entered the top level of the atrium of the exclusive hotel and were greeted by a small army of staff, with one woman announcing herself as their personal concierge. With their destination being the penthouse, it wasn't too long a journey, but she tried to hide the flare of awareness in her body as the concierge directed them towards the open doors of the private lift.

'I'd prefer to take the stairs, please.'

She caught the sudden tightening of his jaw and swore she could feel the heat of his gaze upon her back as she pulled from his grip and walked ahead of him, descending two short flights of stairs to a floor with a single doorway. Was he thinking of that night in the lift, just as she was? Had it haunted him just as it had haunted her?

She was barely aware of Apollo ordering dinner for them both as the double doors were opened and she was met with the most stunning apartment she'd ever seen. The hall alone had to be the size of the entire ground floor of her little London townhouse, and every spare inch seemed to be decorated with priceless paintings and polished marble.

'A literal palace would be less extra than this place,' she half-whispered to herself.

'You think this is extra, you should see the master bedroom.' A husky murmur interrupted her thoughts and she spun to face Apollo, realising they were now alone.

'I don't know what kind of games you're playing, bringing me back to Venice. But it's not going to work. We *will* be discussing your ownership of Accardi and forming a plan.'

She was stalling as she tried to compose herself enough to tell him about the small matter of him having a secret son he'd never known about, but she could only fight one fire at a time. And truthfully, after speaking with Allegra and remembering just what kind of wealth Apollo came from, she felt even more fearful about disclosing her discovery.

Would he even believe her?

Apollo walked past her, disappearing through an arch into the next room. She followed along behind him, her much shorter legs taking twice the time to match his long, even pace as he strode towards a sunken sofa area in the middle of a lavish entertaining space. With a single touch of his hand to a panel on the wall, the lights dimmed and a large fire flared to life. A fully stocked bar rose from the centre of the coffee table, filled with gleaming crystal glassware and pretty much every drink imaginable.

He raised a brow in her direction, grabbing a set of glasses and a bottle of red wine that looked expensive.

'I'm not here to drink with you,' she said tautly, trying to ignore the flare of heat in her stomach at the way his strong hands uncorked the bottle—hands that she remembered working magic on her touch-starved body that night in the dark. Their time together had been fleeting… yet she thought she'd never felt so at ease with another human being.

Before that night, she'd wondered if breaking off her engagement had been a mistake. If maybe all couples had to force things in conversation and in the bedroom. She'd briefly toyed with the idea of going back to playing the part of the good daughter, if only to stop her politician father's cold anger towards her as he'd tried to save face with his constituents in their town because of her having jilted Ian, supposedly the perfect fiancé.

But, after meeting her masked stranger, she'd felt a fierce spark awaken within her. She'd known then that she had made the right choice in wanting more for herself. Even before she'd discovered her pregnancy, just one encounter with this man had changed her whole world. Now, she was about to give him information that would do the same for him.

'Let's get business out of the way first, shall we?' Apollo said, interrupting her thoughts as he slid a glass toward her. 'I always planned to discuss the inheritance with you, but I broke my contract on advice from my lawyers.'

Sighing aloud, she sat heavily on the opposite side of the U-shaped sofa. She took a sip of the wine and barely avoided moaning with satisfaction at the rich, earthy flavour on her tongue. ‘Legally, is there no way that you can own another team and still be a driver for Falco Roux?’

‘They’re not sure yet. It’s unprecedented.’ He sipped from his own glass, a faraway look in his dark eyes. ‘The rumours were true that I left Accardi due to a disagreement between myself and my grandfather. He was a proud man, as underhanded and ruthless as the press made him out to be. Still, I idolised him as a boy. He was the one constant in my life during my parents’ divorce. He spent more time with me than my own father, introduced me to karting, trained me up and channelled my hurt feelings into something positive.

‘But as I grew up I saw a different side of him. I disagreed with many of his team tactics and that was a large part of why I walked away from Elite One for so many years. Still, for some reason he decided to make me his sole beneficiary. Everyone assumed that my cousins would inherit, considering they all three hold important positions in the team.’

Astrid felt her breath catch at the remorse in Apollo’s eyes. She didn’t dare speak, waiting for him to continue, even as she began to realise what his admission was revealing.

‘I never wanted to leave Elite One. I left because I found out secrets within Accardi Autosport that had been meant to be kept hidden from me. Secrets that threw doubt upon all of my successes as a driver for that team. The corrupt deals and moves that Enzo had made in Elite One was only part of the rot that filtered from the top down.

I ran away. I made my own fortune, tried to clear my conscience. Then, when that didn't work, I came back to win the championship on my own terms. Which is what I planned to do, until this happened. I now have an opportunity to step in and put an end to Nonno's legacy of corruption. Not just to prove myself, but to pave the way for the next generation.'

Astrid felt her heart sink. 'And that's what you want?'

'I don't *want* to do it, Astrid.' Apollo practically growled as he stood, looming over her. 'You think I want to be a team owner? I just want to race. I never wanted to be pulled into the family business in that capacity.'

'You could sell the team.' She stood her ground without faltering, far too used to standing toe to toe with hot-headed drivers.

Apollo sighed, sitting back down and finishing the end of his drink with one smooth swallow. He stared at her. 'My grandfather locked down any chance of a sale for five years after my inheritance. My cousins still hold minor shares, and they've made it clear they plan to contest the will, if they can. Allegra and her brothers are leading the movement; they're furious that my grandfather left them nothing in the will.'

'That's what the argument after the funeral was about?'

He nodded. 'People like them…they fear change. They wish the team to continue on as it always has, that's why they want to inherit it. A part of me wants to find a way out, to have nothing to do with any of it. But another part of me feels that I have a duty to undo the legacy of corruption and discrimination at Accardi…that maybe it's time for the team to accept some consequences. And maybe I'm the only one who will do what needs to be done.'

'You really believe that's your responsibility?' Astrid asked gently.

'I walked away from it all once,' he said coolly. 'I don't think I can do it again.'

Astrid knew all about the work Apollo had started before he'd left Elite One. His outspoken call for diversity and inclusion had paved the way for people like Grayson and Nina to set up academies and initiatives of their own, and set real progress in action to remove the many prejudices that so often blocked access to the sport for so many people. Still, they had a long way to go.

She felt unease rise within her at the knowledge that she had failed at the task Tristan had set her to stop him from breaking his contract. There was no way to spin this kind of news. Unless, of course, it became overshadowed by an even more shocking personal revelation.

She closed her eyes, grappling with the other reason she'd come here with him. Every passing moment she didn't tell him about Luca was a weight upon her conscience. Her thoughts raced as she paced to the other side of the room.

'For what it's worth, you were the first person I thought of when I realised I needed to break my contract.' Apollo's gaze heated as it skimmed down the length of her body for the briefest moment. 'Although, not for noble reasons.'

She froze. 'There are some other things we should speak about, Apollo.'

'Let's step away from the serious stuff for a moment,' he murmured. 'See, I've spent the past year respecting your "no drivers" rule…only to find out we already broke it all those years ago. I've thought of nothing but breaking it again all day long.'

'We shouldn't.' She straightened, placing her wine glass down on the table with shaking fingers. She had done her best to keep away from this man for the past year and the strange nervous energy she felt in his presence. He made her feel too much. He made her want too much. She closed her eyes, trying and failing to get a handle on her rapidly scrambling train of thought and ignore how delicious he smelled as he slowly encroached into her personal space. She had to control this situation; she had to tell him what needed to be said and let them both deal with the fallout.

'Do you remember our first kiss, Astrid?' His low whisper was wicked. 'Do you remember how clumsy we were in the dark?'

'Yes,' she heard herself answer. 'We bumped foreheads a couple times.'

'I had a small bruise the next day.' He smirked, leaning closer. 'I told myself, if I ever found you again, that I'd do it right. I'd kiss you slow and perfect, like you deserved.'

In the glow of the fire, she watched him lick his lips with exaggerated slowness and she suddenly *needed* to kiss him again, to know that she wasn't alone in feeling this crawling need that refused to shift whenever they were around one another.

When he reached out and gripped her hips, she nudged closer. When he urged her down sideways onto his lap, she obeyed and heard a sound somewhere between a sigh and a moan escape her lips right before his lips claimed hers.

Apollo almost gave a roar of triumph as he took his fill of Astrid's soft mouth. He kissed her in slow tastes at first, savouring the fact that he'd finally got her right where he wanted. His hands traced a slow path up the soft curve of her hip until he cupped the underside of her breast through the material of her shirt. It was chaste and nowhere near enough, a fact he knew she felt too, as she pushed herself against him, seeking relief but not finding any.

He fought the urge to rip the garment from her skin, slowly unbuttoning the front of her blouse and letting it slide down over her shoulders. Her bra was white lace, and he ached to remove that too, but they had time, he reminded himself. They'd have the entire night this time, if he had his way.

She straddled him fully now, her skirt bunched high up on her hips. The heat of her core was right…there….separated only by the thin layer of her underwear. With her lips devouring his and her soft bottom filling his hands, he had to fight not to thrust up hard as they ground against one another, her tiny gasps of breath indicating she was just as eager to find her pleasure too. It was the hottest thing he had ever seen.

His memory of his mystery woman's sounds in the dark from that long-ago night was nothing compared to seeing Astrid Lewis beginning to come apart in his arms in the present. He'd thought perhaps he'd exaggerated his recollection of the powerful desire he'd felt in that darkened lift; that her walking away from him before he'd had his fill of her had been the reason he'd not been able to shake the thoughts of her for years afterwards. Their encounter had been short, but the chemistry had been as undeniable then as it was now.

The soft lamplight illuminated her fair skin, pink spots high on her cheeks as she moaned her approval and rubbed herself against the hard ridge of his jeans-covered erection. Apollo thought his eyes might roll back in his head from the pleasure of it.

Dio, if he was already being driven wild by this, how on earth would he last inside her? The fact that they were both almost fully clothed only seemed to intensify the sensations and he was powerless not to match her thrusts with his own greedy ones, a rough groan escaping his throat as she increased her pace.

He had been in control of this seduction mere moments before; he'd been sure of it. But now, as he lost himself in the sensation of her softness gliding against him, he felt dangerously close to the edge. He'd never lost it this way, not even in his twenties. Now, at the grand age of almost thirty-three, the very idea of not being able to maintain control for long enough to give his partner an orgasm seemed ridiculous. But here, feeling the heat build behind the zip of his jeans, he understood.

Adjusting her on his lap, he used his hand as a barrier between himself and her sweet heat and he slid one digit along the centre of the delicate lacy scrap of neon-pink silk. The material was already damp and he knew she must be close.

'You're shaking, *carina*,' he crooned against her ear, nipping the lobe gently with his teeth and glorying in her hiss of breath. 'You need release so badly, don't you?'

'Yes.' She breathed the word on a groan, her body instinctively pressing against his touch as he replicated the jerking up-and-back motion she seemed to like. Her eyes widened and he smiled, fighting the urge to make a cocky comment about racing drivers and quick observation skills. Now was not the time for joking, not when she was beginning to shake and shudder so prettily under his touch.

He slowed down as he felt her thighs tighten around him, his eyes never leaving hers as he sucked one pert nipple into his mouth through her bra and bit down hard. She broke apart spectacularly in a cascade of ripples and shakes. The soft breathy cry of, 'Apollo!' was like heaven in his ears, her polished accent so dirty and divine all at once. As she fell forward onto his chest, he swore it wouldn't be the last time she called out his name like a prayer.

He needed more. He needed all of her.

'I want you completely bare to me,' he murmured against her breasts. 'I want no secrets between us.'

Astrid paused, feeling the warmth of her orgasm cool at his words. *Secrets...* She moved backwards off Apollo's lap until she could stand up. Shaky fingers hastily straightened her skirt to hide her still trembling thighs from his hungry gaze.

He licked his lips, moving forward as though he planned to touch her. Instinctively, Astrid stepped out of reach and gulped in a cool breath of air, wondering how on earth she'd just lost control so spectacularly.

She hadn't avoided the final part of her revelation from him on purpose, she'd just got swept away. But would he see it that way? She should have told him about Luca immediately. Damn it.

She blew out another breath in an effort to calm her racing heartbeat and treacherous libido. Her body very much wanted to continue what they'd just begun, a fact that Apollo was quite aware of as he stood up and prowled towards her in the soft light. His hands slid up her arms, then immediately paused as she stiffened under his touch.

'You can't even look at me now?' he said roughly. 'What have I done? Did you not want to—?'

'I wanted to,' she said, pulling out of his touch and crossing her arms over her chest to stop herself from falling back into his strong embrace. What on earth was wrong with her?

'But there are things you need to know. Something I should have told you today.'

'There's nothing you could tell me that would make me not want to do exactly what I just described, Astrid.'

'You might reconsider that in a moment.' She let out a weak attempt at laughter, steeling herself as she met his gaze. 'I told you that I wanted to remain anonymous that night and I did. I didn't start searching for you until eight weeks later, by which time you'd completely disappeared. I even saved up and hired a private investigator.'

'That's bordering on a little obsessive, *bellezza*, but I'd be lying if I said I hadn't tried various avenues to find you too.' He sat back on the sofa, his strong arms spread wide and his eyes still dark with need. 'So long as it leads us both back to the same place—preferably my bed, this time.'

She inhaled a shaky breath. 'I didn't try to find you to get back into your bed, Apollo.'

He quirked one dark brow. 'No?'

'No.' She forced herself to meet his eyes, to get the words out in a way that didn't make her feel as unhinged as she felt inside. 'I needed to find you…to tell you that I was pregnant.'

CHAPTER SIX

ASTRID WATCHED AS Apollo's sultry smirk froze into one of shock, his large, firm body visibly withdrawing a few inches from hers on the sofa. 'You were…'

'Pregnant, yes. With your child.'

He seemed frozen in time, his hands braced on his knees as though holding on for dear life. She felt as if she was diving into her revelation all at once, trying to get it all out before she completely lost her nerve under his scrutiny, so she continued.

'Once I found out and I knew I wanted to keep the baby, I tried to track you down. I had nothing else to go by, other than your basic description that night and the scar on your groin. Nothing solid enough.'

The look on his face was frozen halfway between amusement and horror. The silence was prolonged and painful as Astrid grabbed her shirt from the floor and hastily did up as many buttons as she could manage. When Apollo still made no move to respond, she produced her phone from her bag, clicking a few times until she drew up a photograph, and extended the bright screen towards him. 'He's nearly seven…and his name is Luca.'

Time seemed to move in slow motion as Apollo took in the boy's smiling face, and she watched the play of emotions change from confusion and disbelief to, eventually, awe.

The picture she'd chosen was from a couple of weeks ago, on the last day of school. The sun shone on Luca's little face as he took off down the biggest slide in the playground where they often stopped on the walk home. Short dark curls framed her son's heart-shaped face and his wide toothy grin emphasised the sharp dimple in his little chin—a dimple identical to Apollo's, she realised. How had she not noticed the small similarities? She'd been too busy avoiding her very confusing and improper attraction to one of her drivers that she'd missed what had been right in front of her face.

'You're sure?' Apollo's voice was deeper than usual. 'He's mine?'

There was no accusation in his tone or animosity; in fact he seemed unnaturally calm for a man who'd just been told he was a father. That one word, 'mine', sent a small trigger of alarm through her but she shook it off. She nodded. 'He is your son.'

He remained silent for a long moment and Astrid tried not to fidget under his gaze. 'We used a condom that night, I know. But it was dark and…it must have failed.'

'There was no one else?' he asked.

She shook her head, watching as his eyes darkened with some unnamed emotion before he turned away from her. She didn't expand on that fact; there was no need for him to know that there had been no one else since him, either. He definitely did not need to know that embarrassing fact. But perhaps he might have guessed at the length of her celibacy after how quickly she'd just come apart in his arms after only a few minutes of frantic touches.

She'd been so hypersensitive and lost to his touch that standing alone in the middle of the room had felt like a rush of cold water in comparison.

She waited as he silently processed her words, her body unconsciously braced for the uncertainty of his reaction. He was a powerful man, and she was here alone with him in his cavernous home, but she was not afraid. Whatever happened, she didn't believe he would react to her bombshell with anger, the way her own father had. Sure, he might deny everything she'd just said, or perhaps demand lawyers and a paternity test. Even if it came to that, she'd know she'd done the right thing.

But after a moment, Apollo's eyes raised, pinning her in place with an almost painful intensity.

'You realised this earlier, in Lake Como. When I was in the ice bath.' His eyes met hers, his stunned shock gone, replaced by something darker. 'You discovered something of this magnitude...and you immediately tried to run away from me?'

'I didn't plan to run away.' She bristled. 'I saw your scar, and that tattoo you'd mentioned you wanted, and I just...panicked.'

She blew out a breath, looking around the luxurious apartment that was so very different from her modest home. 'I have a little boy who relies solely on me for stability; what would happen if I just went around accusing Elite One drivers of fathering my son without proof?'

He stood up, moving towards her. 'And you're sure now?'

'I saw the golden helmet statue from that night and I knew it was you without any doubt.' She stood her ground when he came to a stop mere inches from her. 'I knew you were Luca's father.'

His jaw tightened at the last word, his brows furrowing as though he was in pain. She let him think, knowing she'd had an entire afternoon's head start on processing all of this. It was a lot to take in and, while discovering the identity of her child's father had been a shock for her, she couldn't imagine it was any easier to be landed with the existence of an entire child he'd never known existed.

'Are you okay?' she asked softly. 'I know this is a lot to take in.'

'That's quite the understatement,' he said with a frown. 'All day, we've been talking about work. About me inheriting Accardi Autosport and potential media fallouts… Meanwhile, you were hiding this.'

'I wasn't hiding anything. I searched for Luca's father, for you, from the moment I knew I was pregnant. I never dreamed it would be someone in Elite One, someone I've been working with over the past year.'

She closed her eyes, pained once again by the cruelty of it, just as she had been all day. They'd lost so much time. Apollo had missed so much. 'I promise, the moment I realised it was you, I planned to tell you. I wanted us to be alone, to give you time to process everything. There's no manual on how to disclose paternity to someone you had one encounter with in a darkened lift several years ago.'

Apollo was still standing statue-like in the centre of the room and the desolate look in his eyes was beginning to make her feel more than a little uneasy.

'Has he ever asked about his f-father?' he said finally.

That heartbreaking question cut through her as his

voice stumbled slightly over the last word. She'd never heard Apollo Accardi stumble over anything; the man was carved from brazen confidence. She slid her damp palms down along her skirt before answering. 'Yes. Many times.'

'And what did you tell him?'

'That his dad lived somewhere far away and didn't know about him yet,' she answered truthfully. 'Luca was diagnosed with autism a year or so ago. He's a very literal child. I could never lie to him, as he asks follow-up questions and remembers everything.'

She watched as Apollo stared at the phone screen once more, his eyes tracing over the face of the little boy he'd never met. She felt compelled to keep talking, so she told him more about Luca's favourite hobbies and interests—how deeply he adored public transport vehicles at the moment, but how last year it had been dinosaurs and then sharks the year before that. It felt strange, sharing details about her son like this, but at the same time it felt right in a way that scared her senseless.

Apollo drank in every detail Astrid gave so easily about this little boy who was a stranger to him. He wasn't sure how he withstood the earthquake of emotion taking place inside his chest. He stood up and walked to the window of the living room, looking out at the night skyline of Venice spread out below. He closed his eyes, taking a moment to let the last ripples of shock pulse through him.

He had a son. Luca.

'You've raised him alone this entire time?' he heard himself ask, hating that he had to ask such questions about his own flesh and blood. He knew so little about him, and felt himself grabbing onto every piece of information like rare treasure.

'We had some wonderful nannies, and I was able to bring him to race weekends with me thanks to his godfather, Grayson Koh. Grayson is actually married to Luca's old nanny Izzy now. They're like our family.'

He felt a flash of jealousy at the mention of Grayson Koh, an older driver and one of his biggest rivals from his early racing days. He ran a hand through his hair, pushing away the discomfort at knowing the other man had been there for all the moments with Astrid and Luca that he'd missed. He was glad she had not been completely without support. Still, he had to wonder how on earth this had happened. How had they not found one another when they'd both looked? Astrid had said she'd even hired a private investigator. Was it a simple twist of fate that had kept them apart or a more deliberate outside force? His mind turned over the information, something feeling off.

Her phone rang and she froze, uncertainty marring her brow. 'I… I usually video call with Luca every night when I'm away.'

'Answer it.' He sat back against the window ledge. 'I won't announce myself to him over a phone screen, if that's what you're thinking.'

'I don't know what I'm thinking,' she confessed, letting out a breathless sound. 'After today, I don't think I know about anything any more.'

He nodded in understanding, feeling a small moment of solidarity with her in the sea of uncertainty they'd found themselves in. She tapped the screen to answer the call, a small voice with a British accent sounding out loudly in the room.

'Mummy!'

Astrid shifted seamlessly into a soft, loving tone, complimenting something being shown to her on the screen. 'You've tidied your toys up so well, darling. I'm proud of you.'

He was struck by how easily she calmed the child when he became upset, even without him saying any words. She was patient, comforting him with just her voice. Admiration and anger warred within him that she'd had to do all of this alone. She'd raised their son for almost seven years whilst also building a career and a home.

He listened to her gently explain why Luca needed to let the nanny put him to bed, how their plans for their trip tomorrow had changed and she knew that was uncomfortable for him. Apollo moved closer as he heard the small voice repeat her words every few moments and fought the urge to intrude, to demand to speak to his son.

Another voice came onto the phone, a young woman who Astrid greeted as Jem. The girl asked if they could chat about an issue she was having with what sounded like a university application and Astrid's face changed. She gestured to him in apology and quickly excused herself from the room as she switched the phone off speaker mode and listened.

Engulfed in the sudden silence, he found himself filled with nervous energy. Opening his phone, he searched for her name and clicked into social media accounts he'd never seen. He didn't manage his own online presence or spend a lot of time on the Internet, as he hated the waste of time and didn't enjoy the chaotic mix of scrutiny and adoration for his public persona.

There was one website that showed an interview with

Astrid about motherhood and business; a few photographs were included and he took a seat in a wingback chair as he zoomed into each one: Astrid with a rounded bump on the race track; Astrid holding a newborn bundle. He didn't know how long he sat there, scouring through every photo and interview like a starving man, trying to piece together how on earth this had happened.

There were very few photos of Luca on the Internet, and he found himself grateful to Astrid for that, as he realised how important his son's safety was to him. But even the few images of the boy's side profile he'd found on Elite One websites made his chest tighten painfully. His son liked the cars. He could see it in the eager stretch of his small hands over the barriers, and in the official team t-shirts and caps he wore—Accardi caps. A sense of pride filled him, seeing the familiar lettering above the boy's face: his family's name. His son was an Accardi by blood. He should have been the one holding him as they watched the racing, just as his grandfather had done with him when he'd been a boy.

Adrenaline thrummed through him, as if he wanted to run. But for once it was not to run away, but towards this new dimension of his world that had just been presented to him. He never wanted to let them out of his sight. But, with the press already on his heels, he'd created an even worse mess. He had not planned the damned party yesterday, but he hadn't stopped his father either. He'd known it looked terrible and would draw media attention, but he hadn't cared then. He'd only had himself to worry about, his own image.

Now…he didn't quite know how these things worked but he knew he had a right to see his son. He knew that was what he wanted. He knew he wouldn't hide his son's existence either; he wouldn't miss another moment more as Luca's father than he already had.

He waited another half hour before allowing his impatience to win out and going in search of Astrid, only to find she'd fallen asleep on top of the four-poster bed in his guest room. She was still fully dressed, her phone clutched in her hand. She looked tired, her hair mussed and unpinned in a fashion that reminded him of the kisses they'd shared. Of how quickly she'd come undone in his arms, disproving her claims of being unaffected by the desire between them.

She wasn't physically unaffected, but he knew she'd been serious when she'd said she would never risk her professional reputation for a driver. But he wasn't her driver now…he was her son's father.

He was the man who, unknowingly, had walked away and left a woman pregnant and alone to raise their child for almost seven damned years. He hadn't noticed the condom fail, hadn't run after her and insisted they exchange numbers. He'd been out in the world, racing, building his own brand and travelling, living his life as a carefree bachelor. Meanwhile, she had borne the entire responsibility of the consequences of their actions.

He pulled the blanket up from the bottom of the bed, covering her. He paused for a long moment, his mind poring over the events of the day. She let out a small sound, her face turning away from him, as though even while sleeping she could sense the dangerous nature of his thoughts. He had told her he wouldn't give her the chance to run from him again. He believed her when she said she wouldn't try to keep him from his child, but still he felt a strange sense of possession as he looked down at her.

He inhaled a deep breath and closed the door softly behind him on Astrid's seductively slumbering form. Growing up as he had, the child of acrimoniously divorced parents, he'd long ago made peace with his choice to remain single and child-free. But life had a way of changing the best laid plans.

One thing was certain—his son would not grow up the way he had, torn between two homes. He knew Astrid would fight him, he would expect nothing less, but he had no intention of letting go of a perfectly good chance to make this right.

CHAPTER SEVEN

ASTRID AWOKE DISORIENTATED, her mind taking a moment to process the sound of birds chirping and the smell of coffee. Her last memory was of sleepily clutching her phone to her ear as she'd finished guiding Jem through her upcoming university interview, then saying goodnight to Luca. The phone was now thrown on the opposite side of the bed and the covers were tied around her legs as though she had tossed and turned for the entire night. That would explain the panicked dreams she'd had of being pursued in the dark, she thought as she rose from the bed and felt her muscles ache in response.

She hadn't meant to fall asleep, but she supposed the adrenaline of the day was bound to find her eventually. The very idea that twenty-four hours ago she'd been focused on a simple job and entirely unaware of how starkly her life was about to change was an uncomfortable one. Much like her small son, she wasn't fond of change but, where Luca railed against it and felt the effects acutely, Astrid usually found a way to re-centre herself and find control.

Control was not just something she enjoyed, it was something she required. And it was something she'd had the full privilege of with regard to her son since he'd been born. The memory of the look in Apollo's eyes the night before when he had asked her if Luca had ever asked about his father sent a shiver down her spine as she rose and walked into the bathroom, taking in her sleep-worn expression in the bathroom mirror.

Would he be fair in their approach to co-parenting? Would he want more than she was prepared to give? Worries and 'what if?'s swarmed her thoughts as she stripped off and took a quick shower. Not even the hottest temperature and a shelf of luxury products could assuage the tension in her spine as she absent-mindedly towel dried her short brown locks before twisting them into a sleek chignon.

By the time she'd dressed in her preferred uniform of stretchy pencil skirt and lilac blouse, she'd talked herself through every potential scenario and decided she was being ridiculous to worry so much. Sure, Apollo was insanely wealthy and came from a powerful family, but he was not a villain. With his lifestyle, she highly doubted that he had any intention of fighting her for full custody or anything of the sort. Likely, the best-case scenario that she could hope for was that he wanted a relationship with Luca. That he would want to catch up on the time he'd lost, plan some visits and find a way to see him occasionally.

As for Luca, she only hoped that her son would accept the news that he had a father easily. He loved all things Elite One and his favourite team had always been Accardi. She hoped that shared interest would provide a meeting ground of sorts for father and son. Only time would tell. No matter what Apollo was prepared to offer, she already knew she would do her best to make it work.

How many nights had she lain awake with her infant son wondering what she could have done differently? How many times had she cried in the past year since Luca had started to speak and had begun to ask questions about his father, questions that she'd had absolutely no idea how to answer?

The guilt over her actions in the lift that night and the decision she'd made to keep things anonymous had torn at her, and now here she was with the very man she'd hoped to find. Apollo lived his life in the public eye, so they wouldn't be able to keep this a secret for long. But there was no need to make a public statement just yet. Perhaps once things had settled into a rhythm between them all. She hadn't even begun to think of what Grayson and Izzy would say, finding out that Luca was an Accardi. Or what Tristan and Nina would say, especially in the face of losing their star driver and the media storm that would accompany that news breaking.

But she was a professional, and she had never found a situation she couldn't spin…even if this scandal was her own. Still, she couldn't quite shake the sensation that she stood on a precipice of sorts between her old life and a new one.

She held her shoulders high as she exited the guest room in search of the origin of that delicious coffee scent, following it to a modern kitchen. Apollo stood at the worktop, cradling an espresso cup in his hands when she entered.

'Buongiorno.' His husky greeting was pleasant but she noticed an intensity in his eyes as she moved to accept the identical cup of espresso he'd poured for her.

'Sit down. We need to talk.'

Astrid paused at his serious tone, the cup midway to her lips. An illicit shiver ran down her spine at his deep command, even as the more pragmatic side of her rebelled. She inhaled a breath, turning to face him fully in the bright morning light.

'Okay. I know you likely have a lot of questions about what comes next between us…regarding Luca, I mean.' She took a grateful sip of coffee. 'And I want you to know that I'm open to making a plan for you both to meet and get to know one another…and see where we go from there. But, before we can do that, I think we need to get the media situation with your departure from Falco Roux under control.'

'Astrid.' He sighed and scrubbed a hand over his face.

'Please, hear me out, okay? I've sent out some feelers in the media. We have the opportunity to hold a small press conference this morning if you're open to it. I was in contact with one of the Italian sports stations yesterday and they have submitted a list of questions that I feel would be palatable.'

'There can be no interviews.'

'Apollo, as I've told you, there have to be. We need to act fast in order to get ahead of the situation. Before it gets out to our sponsors and the fans and everything snowballs—'

'It has already been leaked.'

Astrid felt a lead weight in her stomach as she looked down to where his fingers slid a morning newspaper across the marble worktop. Headlines in Italian filled the page in large black typeface. Her own grasp of the language was passable, but there was no need to ask for a translation. Not when a giant photograph of Allegra and

Apollo facing off yesterday at the autodrome accompanied it, with a caricature of the brand logos of Accardi and Falco Roux in competition and Elite One as the referee.

'No.' Astrid breathed, her eyes scanning the passage beneath. 'This is an absolute disaster. I need to call my team; we are going to have to set up something global and get in contact with Elite One. They're likely going to jump at an investigation… Apollo, this is an absolute mess.'

'That's not all.'

He turned her attention to the front of the newspaper; she hadn't realised that the headline she'd been looking at was on the inside cover. The front headline had taken a completely different angle.

Figlio d'amore segreto di Accardi

Her eyes slowly rose to where Apollo stared at her. 'Please tell me this does not mean what I think it means.'

'"Accardi's secret love child",' he confirmed solemnly. 'It's on almost every front page in Italy and making its way further afield very quickly.'

'How?' She shook her head slowly. 'We only just found out ourselves yesterday. How on earth is this even possible? I haven't told anyone but you.'

'Are you asking if I leaked this to the press myself, Astrid?'

She hadn't planned to…but even as she processed that idea she disregarded it. No, he knew too well that this would be the last thing either of them needed. The article had been leaked to a journalist she knew was personally in the pockets of Accardi Autosport, not to mention, the timing and the wording… She knew how the Accardi team operated like the back of her hand. This had come from them.

She thought of the past twenty-four hours—of the way Allegra Accardi had referenced her baby bump; how she'd mentioned Luca. Maybe she had noticed Luca's resemblance to a young Apollo, too. It was madness to think that anyone else might have known about Luca's link to Apollo when even she had not known, surely?

'Your cousins,' she said simply. 'Would they have done something like this in order to force you to break the terms of the will?'

'If they have, they'll pay.' Anger radiated from the stern set of his jaw. 'This is unacceptable. Our son has gone from being completely anonymous to being thrust into the circus of the Accardi family with his name on the front page of every newspaper.'

Our son.

Astrid felt her stomach tighten at those words and how easily he'd said them. Also, how he had thought of Luca's safety first. That had to be a good sign, right? That had to mean that her fears were unfounded. She may be a well-paid PR representative with plenty of connections in the media, but her name did not hold a fraction of the power that Apollo's did when it came to keeping their son safe from something like this.

'I grew up in the media spotlight; it is not something I would wish for him, most certainly not so suddenly. This will escalate into a full-blown media frenzy,' Apollo said grimly. 'Would he be awake yet? Is your home secure?'

Astrid paused, horrified awareness finally snaking its way through her shock. She couldn't quite seem to think straight, not when she knew better than anyone that the paparazzi in London were even more brazen and disrespectful than they were here. Not when she couldn't hold her son in her arms and make sure that he hadn't been frightened by an errant photographer outside their door. Her hands scrambled for her phone, fingers shaking uncontrollably as she tried to scroll to her favourites list to call Jem.

'Astrid.' A warm hand held hers, sliding the phone from her fingers. 'You need to stay calm. I'm already thinking about how we can fix this. Protecting Luca is my top priority.'

'How can you protect him? All they have to do is look up my address! They're probably already there. Oh God, Jem and Luca always go out for a walk in the park first thing in the morning. I have to book a flight, I have to get home.'

'I'm already on top of it,' he said earnestly. 'My jet is waiting for us at the airport; we'll be with him in a matter of hours.'

'Thank you.' She tried to feel relief, but instead felt even more dread coil in her stomach. 'Wait…did you say *we*?'

'I'm coming with you, of course.' He stood up straight. 'I would like to meet my son.'

'Do you think now is the best time?'

'It's as good a time as any, when I've missed the pregnancy and the first nearly seven years of his life, wouldn't you say? I have a lot of time to make up for.' His gaze was cool and measured as he slid her phone across the worktop towards her. 'You realise that you can't stay in London whilst this is happening?'

'We had planned to take a trip over to visit Grayson's place in Ireland. I'm sure we can go early and lie low over there.' She blew out a long breath. 'It's not ideal, but thankfully school doesn't start again for another few weeks.'

'You think it's wise to bring this to their doorstep?'

Astrid swallowed past the lump in her throat. No, it wasn't wise, nor was it fair. Izzy was pregnant with their second child and enjoying some down time at their home in the countryside. While she was sure that their security was top of the range, this disaster wasn't something she felt comfortable landing on them.

'I want you both to stay with me while we're getting this media storm under control. For safety reasons, and for the sake of all of our privacy, the best course of action is to take you both under my protection.'

Astrid froze, shaking her head at his words. 'Your protection? I'm perfectly capable of keeping my own child safe. You're a racing driver, for goodness' sake, not a mob boss.'

'I'm an Accardi,' he said simply. 'Much as I've tried to distance myself from that fact. You're not ignorant of the level of power my grandfather's family holds. I was raised amongst them; I know how to handle situations like this. You may know the media like the back of your hand, but you've never faced a scandal like this. I grew up right in the middle of one.'

Astrid was silent, stewing over his words and the annoying truth they held. It seemed he was more controlling and imperious than she'd given him credit for. Still, she forced herself to nod, muttering her agreement between gritted teeth.

'The Monaco race isn't for four weeks, as you know. I planned to spend the summer break at my home in Grenada. It's private, it's safe and we can make our next plans.'

It wasn't an invitation or a request, and she felt her chest tighten. 'I can't just let you whisk us away to the Caribbean. It's…excessive. Not to mention it would be confusing for Luca.'

'Astrid, look at me.' He took her hands in his. 'Luca hasn't even met me yet and already my family name is putting him under threat. Let me take care of you, both of you—let me shield you from this.'

She ignored the shiver of awareness from his touch, and the reminder that being so close to him invoked from the night before. He was just as new to the revelation that they shared a son as she was.

'Okay,' she heard herself agree. 'We'll go with you.'

She was immensely grateful that Apollo had a private jet. The lack of queues and waiting around, unlike a standard commercial airport, meant that they touched down in London far sooner than she'd anticipated. She realised that with the time difference Luca would only just be finishing his second breakfast of the morning. Without the usual school classes or activities, Jem had been planning to take them both on a trip to the playground, but a quick phone call had forewarned them both to remain indoors with the curtains drawn.

She had asked Apollo to remain behind and allow her some space to pack their things and explain the situation to Luca. There had been an odd tension between them since last night that she couldn't quite place. Of course, things would be tense, considering the shock of discovering they shared a son, but there was something else in the way Apollo looked at her. Something dark and brooding that sent shivers down her spine.

Apollo's jaw had been like steel as he'd cleared her to leave with one of his personal security detail, and she had felt the tension coming off him in waves as he'd remained behind on the private airfield and watched her hire car drive away. She was barely aware of the familiar sights of London passing her by, such was her inner turmoil over the events of the past twenty-four hours. Yesterday, she'd woken up in her normal bedroom with her biggest worry being how to switch off her brain from work for a few weeks. Today she was contemplating co-parenting her precious son with a brooding billionaire.

She wasn't quite sure how or when she would tell Luca about his father, but she had told Apollo they needed to take it slowly. A sudden revelation would not be well received by Luca right now, especially after his plans had already had to change so much this week.

Her son's frown greeted her when she finally walked into their townhouse, his eyes shrewdly taking in her rumpled appearance and likely quite tired expression. After a tight hug, his favourite, she sat down with him on the sofa and told him that their trip to Ireland would become an adventure to a brand-new place with lots of beaches. Predictably, he was not amused.

'Don't like new,' he said softly, tears forming in his green eyes.

'New can be fun,' she tried, noting Jem's wince from across the room. 'I'm sorry, darling; are you very disappointed?'

A single nod was his only answer.

'It's okay to have big feelings. I've had big feelings

too.' She patted his back softly. 'But I promise you, it will be fun. Plans change sometimes.'

Luca stood up and moved to the small swing chair they kept for him in the living room, as the movement helped him to regulate his bigger emotions. With a scowl and a huff, he sat down into the stretchy material and solemnly swung his legs.

'We'll be going there on a private jet.' She continued to speak, deciding to take a different tactic. 'Not a normal plane, one of the *fancy* ones with big sofa seats. You'll even have your own bedroom on it.'

Another solemn nod, but no further arguments, which was always a good sign. She took another look at her son and noticed just how much he had already grown this summer. His legs had become long and gangly and his cheekbones had lost some of their baby fat.

How long could she continue to call him her *little* boy? How much of this situation would he understand? From experience, she knew he understood and pieced together things much faster than other children his age. She closed her eyes and let out a long sigh.

'Mummy is feeling sad,' Luca said matter-of-factly, mimicking her sigh with one of his own, much to her amusement.

'Mummy is feeling a little tired,' Astrid corrected with a weak attempt at a smile. 'Mummy also doesn't like it when plans change, just like Luca.'

'Will be fun,' he said patting her softly on the knee. 'Plans change, darling.'

She chuckled out loud and heard Jem's equally amused burst of laughter from the opposite sofa. They had waited so long, wondering if Luca would ever talk. Some called his type of speech a form of mirroring or scripting, and he was selective about when he opted to use verbal communication. But every small gesture or sound he used to make his voice heard would always be something she treasured. When he stood up and began to chuck some of his toys into his rucksack, she knew he was over his disappointment for now. Evidently, the promise of a bedroom on an aeroplane was bribery enough to ensure his cooperation.

As they finished getting ready and said goodbye to Jem, Astrid wondered if perhaps Luca might be taking this situation better than his mother was. There was only one way to find out.

Apollo couldn't remember feeling more nervous in his life. After taking a small trip to gather some items he deemed immediately necessary, he had returned to the jet even more uncertain as he surveyed the parcels he'd accumulated. As he surveyed the small mountain of transport-themed toys and books piled up at the rear end of the jet, he wondered if perhaps he might have gone a little overboard. There was no time for him to rethink his plan, however, as through the plane window he spied their arrival.

Usually, nerves like this could threaten to overcome him as he sat in a car on the grid, listening to his team in his earpiece and going through his strategy for the race ahead. No matter what sport he had moved to over the past seven years or so, his strong internal focus had always centred him in the face of uncertainty. But it seemed that there was no script he could use for this, because the breath immediately left his lungs when Astrid stepped out of the car and he got the first look at his son's face.

The little boy took an uncertain step out into the midday sunshine, his dark springy curls hanging low on his forehead as he bounced on the balls of his feet. Astrid held him by the hand but he made quick work of pulling away and racing directly towards the spot where Apollo had just reached the bottom step of the stairs.

'You are Apollo Accardi,' the small voice proclaimed, stopping a couple of steps away from him with a serious look on his small face.

Apollo froze in place, not quite knowing whether to say anything at all, after Astrid's insistence that they needed to wait before telling him that Apollo was his father. But he'd suspected that Luca would already recognise him to a certain degree. The little boy knew all the Elite One drivers from watching the races.

'I know your name too, Luca. I've been very excited to meet you.'

Luca blinked in his direction, his small fingers twisting by his sides as he looked past Apollo to take in the impressive jet behind him. Transport…*right.*

'We will be flying to Grenada, where some of our…*my* family is from.' Apollo swallowed hard at his near miss, feeling Astrid's gaze heavy upon him. Perhaps he should have stayed inside and allowed them to situate themselves at their own pace, he thought. Perhaps he was already messing this up… But, just as he was poised to turn round and give them space, he felt a small tug at the bottom of his shirt and looked down to find his son had stepped even closer and was eagerly pointing to the aircraft.

Without missing a beat, Apollo kneeled down and began to name every single detail he could remember about the plane. When that wasn't enough, he called out the pilot, who offered even more detail. By the time they finally got inside the jet, his throat was dry from talking and his heart hammered as if he'd run ten miles, and still the boy tugged on his shirt to move towards the cockpit, not yet satisfied.

Apollo couldn't help but feel that this first meeting was fast slipping out of his control, but then he looked at Astrid and caught the small smile on her lips, and wondered if maybe he hadn't done so badly after all.

CHAPTER EIGHT

PREDICTABLY, LUCA DID not sleep one wink on the eleven-hour flight. With only a four-hour time difference between London and Grenada, they touched down in St. George a little past his bedtime, but not too far past the zones within which he might become overly dysregulated and struggle even more to find sleep. As it happened, Luca's eyes began to droop just as they got into the sleek chauffeur-driven car and made their way along the coastline of the capital city.

With her own eyes dry and aching with tiredness, Astrid felt as if she were in a dream as the car swept through security at a set of impressive gates, leading to a long tree-lined driveway, and the facade of a grand villa came into view. The smell of sea salt and the sound of waves crashing surrounded her as her door was opened and the balmy night breeze invaded the car. Apollo's gaze drifted to where Luca still slumped fully asleep and she saw his brief moment of hesitation.

'Will he wake if I carry him?' he asked.

Astrid shook her head, gently sliding her arm out from under Luca's little body and angling him to a more easily accessible position. A lump formed in her throat as she watched the careful, almost reverential way Apollo lifted his son into his arms for the first time. Their eyes met across the darkness of the car interior and she saw a flash of intense emotion there before he looked away. Their bags were already being brought inside by a small army of housekeeping staff so there was nothing for Astrid to do other than follow Apollo into the grand hall of the impressive villa.

Despite it most certainly being another very large home for one man, she was surprised at the warmth and personality of the interior. Wooden beams and green potted plants added to the general feeling of comfort amongst the colourful modern decor. This home was not like his others; there was no artifice and polish here, no priceless paintings or marble busts of ancient emperors. Instead, the walls contained large canvases and framed photography of…turtles?

In fact, when she looked closer, there were even tiny turtle motifs in the woodwork of the staircase too. As they reached a short corridor on the second floor, she watched the lamplight play on the wide expanse of Apollo's shoulders and noticed that, un-styled, the curls on top of his head were almost identical to Luca's. He guided them into a large bedroom near the end of the hall. They'd barely had a chance to speak throughout most of the flight, with Luca a blur of movement around the cabin. When he had discovered the pile of toys Apollo had purchased, her son had insisted they all sit together and unbox each item one by one.

Much of his communication came in the form of pointing and lifting his preferred grown-up's hands in the direction of the item he wished to look at. It was usually only Astrid or Jem who got his glittering sparkles of sentences. He used spoken language sparingly, though he had proven time and time again that he had a more than average understanding of vocabulary for a boy his age. She had already mentioned that Luca was autistic to Apollo, giving him a few tips to help smooth the way, but she had not elaborated further than that. She wanted Luca to be understood for who he was, rather than being the result of a series of key points from an Internet search.

As far as first meetings went, they'd done brilliantly. For a man who had worried he'd have no idea how to interact with children, Apollo had been gentle and patient, which was all she could ask for. He'd taken her tips on board, of course, but more than that he'd asked Luca questions instead of directing his queries to Astrid, as many others sometimes did. He also hadn't pushed or reacted with disappointment when he hadn't received a spoken answer.

She helped him to get the sleeping boy into bed and they both tip-toed from the room.

'I've had your things brought next door to the master bedroom.'

'Isn't that...*your* bedroom?'

'Usually, yes.' His eyes met hers, a flicker of that same intensity she'd seen downstairs burning bright for just the barest second before he ran a hand through his hair. 'No need to look so nervous, Astrid. I have other guest rooms to choose from.'

'I'm not nervous.'

'Your constant jumping from my touch and attention tells me otherwise.' He sighed. 'But, as I said before, my reasons for bringing you here are mostly practical. And

I thought you'd want to sleep near Luca, considering he's in a new place.'

'That's thoughtful, thank you.' She waited for a breath, feeling awkward in the prolonged silence between them after a day of determinedly disregarding the other tense moments they'd shared during their whirlwind reunion in Italy. Moments that she had already decided could not be repeated if they hoped to co-parent successfully. Sure, she'd ached when she'd remembered coming apart in his arms on that sofa in Venice, and she knew it would be all too easy to lose that control again.

But, whilst Apollo was intent upon building a connection with his son, he'd given no indication that he had any other intentions towards her. He was used to travelling the globe, and was never photographed with the same woman twice. After ending her first relationship, Astrid had decided never again to let a man change her plans. Certainly, since Luca had been born, she'd vowed that if she ever risked another relationship it would only be with someone who slotted into the life she'd built with her son. And, while the idea of casual sex with Apollo Accardi was…incredibly tempting, it was better this way, keeping their relationship focused solely on Luca.

Apollo led her into the master suite, a grand room that had a wall of windows to the front of the property. Inky-black night was all that greeted her when she threw open one door and stared out, but the sound of waves and the smell of sea salt told her that the morning view would be spectacular.

'If you're worried that I'm going to demand you share my bed while we're here, you can relax,' he mumbled. 'Unless, you *want* me to demand it?'

'Of course not!'

'No?' He stepped closer. 'Because in Venice you were all for continuing to explore that part of our little reunion.'

'I wasn't exactly thinking straight then,' she said, fighting the urge to add that she never seemed to think straight around him. Instead, she crossed her arms and straightened her spine in an effort to feel even a modicum of control. 'Apollo, you know that sex would only complicate things between us.'

'Don't you think "complicated" is just another word for exciting?'

'If we have any hope of being successful co-parents, we need to not have any more conflicts of interest between us than there already are.'

'Conflict of interest,' he said darkly. 'That's truly how you see this?'

'I still work for Falco Roux, and you're still dealing with your situation at Elite One. We have a son together.'

'You think all of those things change the fact that we can't go five minutes without wanting to tear one another's clothing off?'

'Contrary to my previous behaviour, I do possess some self-control.' Astrid bit down on her lower lip. 'Already Luca and I have been swept away from London and we're staying here in your home. I won't risk confusing him for the sake of a quick fling.'

'What makes you think it would be quick?' He raised a brow.

'I'm serious; your exciting dating lifestyle isn't something I expect you to change just because you've become a father. Just as I don't plan to change my own. We should keep things clear between us, no complications.'

'Seems like you're well-acquainted with my wild dating history. Care to share yours?'

'Compared to you, there's nothing to share.' She shrugged. 'Once Luca came along, I decided that I wouldn't get involved with anyone unless I knew it could be serious. Since you, there hasn't been anyone.'

'Good.' He turned away, pinching the bridge of his nose. 'I mean, it's good that you know what your boundaries are.'

'I have to.' She shrugged. 'When breaking them affects more than just me.'

Apollo's gaze turned serious. 'I brought you both here to keep you safe and I meant every word—my protection does not come with the condition that you share my bed. In fact, how about this—I give you my solemn word that I will *not* attempt to seduce you.'

'Okay…thank you.' She bit back a smirk, amazed at how he could make such a strange and serious admission playful.

'I respect your need to lay down some ground rules. I mean it: if that's what you want, I won't touch you again.' He walked as far as the door, turning just before he moved out of sight. 'Just remember, I never said that you couldn't break those rules yourself.'

Over the next few days, Apollo appointed himself as their personal tour guide, taking them on day trips to explore the beaches and nature trails that surrounded his property, as well as arranging boat trips to let Luca view the various coastal sights from a comfortable distance as they eased into their new surroundings.

They adapted a new routine, rising early to eat breakfast together on the veranda before packing picnic lunches to bring out on their travels. If Apollo was dissatisfied with her wish not to include visits to some of Grenada's fine dining establishments, he didn't say. Luca's diet was limited to some of his preferred familiar brands which she had been sure to pack enough of, as well as specifically prepared fruits, vegetables and pasta shapes. Astrid, on the other hand, adored food in all its forms but she didn't need to be wined and dined, not when the main point of this trip was for Apollo to get to know their son.

To his credit, he threw himself into being the perfect balance of fun and relaxation, allowing Luca to come to him and wander off or go silent as he saw fit. He asked her questions about Luca and listened attentively to her answers, adapting his approach to the boy when needed. For three days, they spent the majority of their time together, then one day in the late afternoon Apollo disappeared for his second daily training regime at a private gym he frequented while on the island. She knew from previous interviews that he trained both in the morning and evening to maintain his performance as a driver, summer break or not. Despite saying he was no longer a driver, he was still taking his training seriously, which had her clinging to a little foolish hope that he might change his mind about quitting Falco Roux. He wasn't a top athlete in one of the most competitive and demanding sports in the world for no reason. Apollo had the kind of talent and drive that people studied and tried to emulate but never could.

Astrid tried not to feel his absence as she passed the evenings swimming with Luca in the shallow end of the gorgeous saltwater pool and taking turns going down the slide built into a large rock feature. But Apollo didn't return to the house after Luca's bed times. If he did, he didn't make himself known to her or try to seek her out, which was exactly the kind of respectful co-parenting she'd asked of him. He was a grown man on a break from work; they hadn't made any personal plans, nor did he need to report his actions to her.

Once dusk fell on their third night in Grenada and Luca was safely tucked into bed, she wandered along the corridors of the large house, finding yet more turtle designs in the tile patterns and light switches. Finding a comfortable recliner on a cute wooden veranda that overlooked the beach, she took some time to answer the small matter of emails and phone calls she'd been dodging since leaving London.

It seemed that being named as the mother of an Elite One driver's secret love child was causing no small amount of concern for Falco Roux. She had contacted Tristan and Nina to forewarn them, but still, guilt plagued her for not jumping in to help. But it was far too personal for her to remain cool-headed, in her usual manner. She knew she had made the right call, and protecting her son had to take priority in this situation, something she hoped her team would understand. She had just finished typing another long-winded email reply when she became aware of raised voices coming through a set of partially open double doors nearby.

'This whole situation stinks of Enzo's meddling,' a female voice said loudly. 'These things don't just remain secrets without someone ensuring it, Apollo. Can you trust that no one paid the child's mother to stay hidden? Can you trust *her*?'

'That is not your place to question, Mother,' Apollo's deep tone answered.

Mother. Astrid stood from her seat, realising that the woman's voice belonged to none other than famous film director Leona Hart. And they were discussing *her.*

'I'm just saying, there is no way that your *nonno* wasn't aware of what happened if she hired an investigator to find you,' Leona said. 'Every PI in Italy is on Accardi's books.'

'So you were too busy to come to breakfast this morning, but you had plenty of time to go digging into my son's mother's past? Astrid is not to blame for any of this.'

'I'm not blaming her, Apollo. I'm pointing out the disparities in her story. All roads lead to Enzo Accardi.'

'The man is dead.'

'You think that would stop him?'

Apollo let out a harsh laugh. 'Stay in here all you like. Meet your grandson or don't. It was nice seeing you.'

Astrid didn't have a second of warning before the double doors were fully pushed open and Apollo's fuming face took in her guilty pose. One of his dark brows raised. 'Eavesdropping?'

'No,' she said, her cheeks heating. 'Sorry, I didn't mean to, I was just sitting here.'

'You have nothing to apologise for. Isn't that right, Mother?' he said sternly, moving aside as a beautiful woman appeared in the doorway. Leona Hart was a stunning black woman in her fifties, with the kind of statuesque presence that stopped people in their tracks.

'My mother was just leaving; she has an event to attend.'

Apollo turned as his mother sighed and stepped around

him, extending her hand in greeting. 'Lovely to meet you, Astrid. I'm sorry to make a poor first impression. I'm enormously protective of my son…'

'I understand. I feel the same way about my own.' Astrid managed a tight smile as Leona's eyes lowered with understanding. Astrid found herself utterly starstruck by the older woman, having long admired her films. Her directorial debut, a poignant biopic set here on Grenada, had taken the world by storm and she'd won a handful of major awards since. They shared a brief moment of small talk about the various sights Astrid should see while visiting, before Apollo left to escort his mother to where her driver waited to take her to a gala in St George.

Once they'd gone, Astrid stared out at the darkening horizon and tried not to feel a sense of anger at what she'd overheard. She did understand, to a certain degree. Their story was more than a little dramatic and unbelievable. It was quite surreal that they'd both looked for one another, worked in the same industry and likely heard one another's names countless times over the past few years without ever discovering the truth.

But it wasn't her fault, nor was it her son's, and she wouldn't allow anyone to make her feel like some sort of criminal—family or not.

Apollo could see the tension in Astrid's posture as he approached the veranda where she stood looking out at the ocean. It was clear that she adored his villa just as much as he'd hoped she would when he decided to bring her here. But the strength of the obsession he'd felt since she'd laid down her boundaries the night they'd arrived, coupled with the temptation of being near her for the last three days…that he had not foreseen.

Walking downstairs to the sight of Astrid and Luca at his usually empty breakfast table each morning had awakened some kind of primal need within him—a need to claim his son as his own in front of the whole world, and for his son to claim him back.

And as for Luca's mother… His need for her had never been in question. But what she'd said had forced him to think more deeply about what he truly wanted when it came to the prim English beauty who had haunted him for the past year. She'd made it clear she didn't see him as a viable candidate for anything serious. Contrary to her jibes about his love life, he hadn't dated at all since he'd joined Falco Roux; he'd been far too busy focusing on winning and trying not to flirt with her.

She wanted them to put aside the undeniable chemistry between them so that they could…'co-parent platonically'. It had to be the competitive Accardi streak in him that saw her confidence as a challenge.

He didn't think he was capable of doing anything platonically with Astrid Lewis. But did that mean that he was ready for the consequences of pursuing a relationship with the mother of his child? He'd realised over the past few days that was exactly what he wanted. It was the most logical solution for them all. He could not go so far as to allow the fantasy of love to muddy the waters, but with Astrid he didn't think that would be an issue. He would offer her a mutually beneficial arrangement, based on convenience and desire.

He'd seen the results of a fractured love match as a child; he'd been the collateral damage. Astrid herself had said over and over that Luca needed consistency. What could be more consistent than having both of his parents calmly agreeing to live together under the same roof…and in the same bed…without any declarations of love to cloud the issue? She was a logical woman; she would surely see the benefits of becoming his wife? He'd make sure of it.

He made his footsteps a little heavier as he neared where she sat on the veranda, announcing his arrival. She turned towards him warily him and he exhaled a breath at her fresh-faced beauty. Astrid perfectly pinned up and polished had long been a feature of his fantasies, but this relaxed, windswept version was fast becoming a new favourite. She was barefoot and wore a loose pale-blue sundress, and hadn't bothered to blow-dry her hair, letting it fall in loose waves around her face.

'So…that was your mother.' She attempted a light tone, but her eyes remained guarded.

'I believe that her concern comes from the right place, but I have warned her that any…accusations are not to be repeated. That I trust you fully and we are in this together,' he said.

'I appreciate that.'

He wondered at the surprise in her tone, and the way her shoulders had relaxed slightly. Had she expected him to take his mother's side? Had she expected the same level of suspicion from him as well? He felt shame wash over him.

'Astrid, I've never shared my mother's suspicions about you. I feel the need to make that abundantly clear.'

'It wouldn't be beyond reason if you did.' She shook her head, turning back to look out at the rapidly darkening sky. 'I knew I did my best to find Luca's father. But maybe she's right about there being a reason why I hit a roadblock in finding you. Maybe someone deliberately placed it there.'

Apollo's jaw tightened, knowing that the same thought had plagued him for the past few days as well. It didn't make sense; even with privacy laws, any decent private investigator would have been able to discover who had been renting the penthouse in the Venice hotel that night. He remembered how Allegra had mentioned Luca at the track and the nugget of suspicion in his gut grew further. He knew there were more questions he needed to ask.

'My father's family don't have the best track record when it comes to honesty,' he said bitterly, noting Astrid's immediate wince at his unintentional pun.

'That's an understatement.'

'I'd like to think that their tricks and underhanded dealings are strictly reserved for racing...but perhaps not.'

'The timing is a little too perfect for coincidence. Coming at it from a PR perspective, if I were Allegra Accardi right now, and I had any kind of information that would discredit you, overwhelming you with bad press would be a great way to try and get control of a team that's already in flux, no?'

Apollo nodded, hearing what she said and knowing she was right. If Enzo had known how ruthless his only granddaughter could truly be, maybe he would have left her the team instead.

Apollo had put his entire reputation on the line only to find out that his grandfather had been cheating and that his first and only drivers' championship win had been sullied by the revelation of espionage against another team. The realisation had shattered many of his illusions about himself and the family who had raised him, and spurred him to distance himself from them entirely. He would never know if he'd still have beaten Grayson Koh in that championship without Enzo's meddling, but it didn't matter, because that win was worthless to him as a result.

He'd spent as much time as he could here on the island since he'd walked away from Elite One, building this villa and the surrounding nature reserve with his own two hands and reconnecting with his mother. He'd still flown round the world to try his hand at various motor sports, just to prove to himself that it wasn't just his grandfather's influence that had made him a success. He'd then focused on growing his 'Apollo' sports brand, which had succeeded beyond his wildest expectations.

To think, during all of that time, Astrid had been growing their son, giving birth to him alone and figuring out how to raise him. He'd missed so many of those first moments a father was supposed to be present for. Thanks to a love of parties and a penchant for sleeping with his co-stars, Santo Accardi had been inconsistent at best during the tumultuous years of Apollo's childhood. When it came to choosing between fame or parenting moments, his father had always preferred the spotlight and accolades.

He turned away, scowling out at the horizon.

His plan to spend his time here getting to know his son and exploring his chemistry with Astrid had seemed so simple at the start. Then, he'd decided that there was only one logical solution to their secret love-child dilemma: for he and Astrid to marry. He'd seen her ground rules as a challenge and prepared himself to regroup and begin again from a different angle. He was no stranger to changing tactics and starting over with a fresh plan of action in the face of difficulty…

But, as he stared down at Astrid's worried face, he suddenly saw all of this from her perspective. Her life was in chaos, and the world she'd built as a single mother for her young son was being threatened. He had barely known of his son's existence for more than twenty-four hours before he'd essentially caused their orderly life to implode.

He had grown up indoctrinated into the importance of what it meant to be an Accardi. Did he really believe it was the best course of action to have his son become one too? Or was that simply his own selfish nature and arrogance at play?

'Apollo?'

Astrid's worried tone jolted him from his thoughts and he tried to remember what they'd been discussing. 'Let me handle Falco Roux and Allegra. I brought you here to let you regroup in privacy, not monopolise your PR skills.'

'My skills are currently useless, considering Tristan Falco has essentially put me on suspension.'

Apollo stilled. 'He did *what*?'

'Not as a punishment or anything; it's more that my ability to quell any media storm is only useful to the team when I myself am not a large moving piece of the scandal.'

Apollo narrowed his eyes. He'd avoided Falco's calls thus far out of necessity, on advice from his legal team, but perhaps he needed to remind his ex-boss of a few choice facts.

He might not have had anything to do with the media storm they found themselves in, but he hadn't been proactive enough in ensuring his son's existence was kept secret. One thing was for sure, his desire to connect with his son could not come before his duty to protect him from harm—protect Astrid too. He'd allowed his judgement to become clouded with idealism and the desire to put the past seven years to rights, but he hadn't considered that perhaps Luca's distance from the tangled web of the Accardi family had been a gift in itself.

'You didn't cause this scandal, Astrid. I will not allow you or Luca to be punished because of my family's machinations.' He took a deep breath and turned, disappearing back into his study and closing the door firmly behind him.

CHAPTER NINE

ASTRID SAW APOLLO again the following morning when they spent time with Luca at the pool. He was keeping his distance from her, avoiding all talk of Falco Roux and his dealings with Accardi, which she supposed she should be grateful for, considering she was clearly biased in wanting him to remain in his current contract. She heard his voice raised in the afternoon as he took various online meetings.

She hadn't spent the day moping, of course; she'd thrown herself into making memories with Luca—building sandcastles on the beach and trying to spot turtles in the bay. Her son's boundless energy was well suited to island life, with the ample sunshine and nature providing the perfect environment in which he could be his wild, curious self.

Apollo's mother returned the next day to apologise for the unpleasant altercation during their first meeting. She asked to meet Luca, introducing herself simply as Leona and asking him if he would like to play chess. Every young boy should play chess, she had declared, sweeping him over to an ornate table in the corner of their dining room and proceeding to spend an hour explaining the game in detail over and over, at Luca's request. She and Apollo had watched from the sofa and Astrid had joked that it seemed Luca had got his competitive streak from both of them. That made a strange smile cross Apollo's face before he promptly remembered he had a call to make and excused himself.

Leona had returned each day for the rest of the week, spending her afternoons with them as though she couldn't quite stay away. The look of adoration on the older woman's face as she interacted with Luca, never wavering in her patience, made tears come to Astrid's eyes on more than one occasion. She surprised the older woman with a virtual baby album she kept saved in her cloud storage, and held Leona's hand as the tears fell from both of their eyes.

'I would have liked to hold my grandson as a baby, to watch him grow,' Leona said sadly. 'But you did a beautiful job of it all by yourself. Well done, darling.'

The hug that followed was so real, so all-consuming, that Astrid had to excuse herself to the bathroom and quietly weep. She had never truly grieved the loss of her own parents' support as she'd become a mother and raised Luca all alone. Their traditional beliefs had formed a barrier in their relationship, long before their cruel abandonment of her after she'd become pregnant had estranged them for good. Her own mother would never have hugged her, or complimented her; she just hadn't been a warm, loving person. Hearing such maternal words of affirmation and recognition from a woman she admired… It struck something within her.

By some strange twist of fate, they discovered that Luca's seventh birthday fell on the same day as Apollo's, a fact that made Leona's eyes tear up as she asked if she might throw her grandson a birthday party.

Astrid didn't usually over-indulge her son, preferring to keep his gifts simple. But when she found that Apollo had collected a small mountain of perfectly wrapped gifts in his study, she felt panicked at her own lack of preparation. She told him this when he quizzed her sudden apprehension, and within an hour he had arranged for a driver to take the three of them into the city of St George for a quick shopping trip.

Grenada's capital was a picturesque city with red-tile-roofed shops and homes dotting the hillside of an old volcano crater. She took a small detour, taking in the beautiful horseshoe-shaped harbour and yacht lagoon, and noting the sight of cruise liners from all over the world far out in the bay. The architecture was an eclectic mix of colonial styles with English, French and West Indian influence visible.

She almost wished she had more time to wander as she smelled the fabulous food, and slowed down past various restaurants and takeaway spots. Some higher end restaurants were also scattered around, offering a variety of international cuisines, but the creative local cuisine smelled the best. One sign proclaimed Grenada's national dish—oil down—a one-pot meal featuring salted meat, chicken, dumplings, breadfruit and callaloo. Fresh local seafood, other fresh produce and meats prepared with true West Indian flare were offered from market stalls and shop fronts by friendly sellers and it seemed as if every stall offered the famous nutmeg ice-cream, the smell making her mouth water.

She aimed to be quick, so as not to leave Luca for too long, but she soon lost herself in the joy of scanning the shelves and stall-fronts as she selected gifts for Luca and some small trinkets to bring home for Jem too. She adored gift-giving, much more than receiving. But, when it came to selecting something for Apollo, she came up short. What on earth did one buy for a man who could purchase an entire island on a whim? She settled upon a pair of carved turtle cufflinks, hoping he would at the very least appreciate the gesture, then went back in search of them in the now much busier afternoon crowd.

In hindsight, she realised she possibly should have left Luca at the villa, as the city was becoming increasingly loud with the build up to the annual carnival celebrations. She panicked when she couldn't immediately find them, but needn't have worried, as Apollo stood in a quiet spot at the edge of the town square with Luca up on his shoulders as they watched a traditional Grenadian costume parade of colourful dances. Performers in elaborate outfits pranced around whooping and hollering, much to the glee of the crowds that lined the streets.

The moment Luca spotted her, his little face crumpled up and he began to cry. Guilt piled upon her as Apollo's face looked shellshocked at the sudden change in their son. Without delay, they moved away from the noise and back towards the car that waited at the edge of the street for them.

'I thought he was enjoying it,' he said, gently placing the boy in her arms and sliding in alongside her while the driver packed away her shopping bags. Astrid held Luca tightly as he rocked in her lap until he dozed off, exhausted.

'He gets overwhelmed and doesn't realise it sometimes until he sees me or Jem. Like a bottle of fizzy lemonade, the pressure builds up until it explodes.'

Apollo nodded 'I guess that's put a stop to the little surprise I had planned.'

'Surprise?'

'I had him booked into the karting track as a treat.'

Astrid felt her chest tighten. Apollo had seen Luca's interest in his racing memorabilia, and she had told him how much he had enjoyed attending the races before they had moved back to London full-time. But the idea of Luca actually getting into a kart on a real track… 'He's…he's only seven years old.'

'I started when I was five,' Apollo said proudly. 'The younger the better, really, to start the skill building.'

'No.' Astrid shook her head. 'Absolutely not. It's much too dangerous a sport and I'm just not comfortable.'

'You do know what I do for a living, yes?' He attempted a half-smile. 'I think it would be great for him. He's a clever kid, and he already adores the track. You can't keep him wrapped up for ever, and you won't know what he's capable of until you let him try.'

She felt guilty as he walked away but couldn't help it. She'd been working in Elite One for so long; she'd seen so many accidents and how drivers' careers could end in the blink of an eye. Thankfully the safety regulations had come on so much over the past couple of decades that there were very rarely any fatalities or serious injuries, but still, every race had things go wrong; it was unavoidable. It was a high-pressure, high-speed, high-risk sport and that was the reason why the drivers adored it. She had never met a driver who wasn't a complete adrenaline junkie, who didn't love the thrill of it all. It was in their blood.

She sat there for a long while afterwards, mulling his

words over and over. Luca wasn't a daredevil, not really. Of course, she had never actually allowed him to try anything she considered remotely risky… She thought of how proud Leona was of all Apollo's achievements, and how she'd kept every single trophy and memento of his. Leona was a doting mother who also adored her son; she had likely feared for Apollo's safety, but she'd been able to push past it. Was she being selfish in holding Luca back from something he might share with his dad? Was she brave enough to trust Apollo to take the lead?

Apollo had spent almost every birthday here in Grenada and he adored it. This year was entirely different, for obvious reasons, but watching his young son race down the stairs and rip open his birthday gifts held him almost entirely frozen on the sofa.

Luca was a blur of motion as he played with each of the carefully selected gifts Apollo had picked out and showed them to Astrid, and they both smiled at one another and got to assembling the various toys in turn.

Apollo was surprised when Astrid gave him a small wrapped box as a gift; he hadn't expected anything. The velvet interior contained a perfectly detailed pair of carved wooden turtle cufflinks. She'd noticed his mild obsession, it seemed, and something warmed within him at that knowledge.

He took his time getting dressed in a shirt that best set off the small blue stones in the turtle shells, noting her eyes wandered to them with surprise when she saw he'd chosen to wear them immediately. Feeling slightly removed from the festivities once his family began to arrive and a delicious birthday feast was firmly under way, he poised himself to melt away into the background, only for Astrid to stand up and walk to him with another box in her hands, this one square-shaped and much bigger.

'This one is also for you…a last-minute addition.' Her cheeks burned with embarrassment. 'It's not quite as generous as what you've given us—in fact, I'm not even sure if it technically counts as a gift at all—but I wasn't quite sure what to give the man who seems to have everything.'

He ignored that last line, knowing that she couldn't be further from the truth. He tore open the wrapping paper on the box, feeling a solid weight inside. Nothing could have prepared him for what lay inside. He opened the lid and saw the smooth unmistakable red dome of a racing helmet. But not any racing helmet, his own—the very first one he'd ever raced in as a boy. His mother must have given it to her.

'This is…' He didn't quite know what to say, and wasn't sure what she could possibly mean by giving this to him.

'It's more a symbol than a gift, I suppose.' She took a deep breath. 'I want Luca to wear it. Specifically, I want you to give it to Luca, with my blessing.'

'Your blessing…for me to take him karting?'

'Yes,' she said, her hands twisting together. 'I overreacted yesterday to your plans and I realised that it was my own fear standing in the way of a bond I very much wish you to have with him. He's a very lucky boy to have such a talented father, one who wants to take the time to share in his interests.'

'My mother had the same reservations when my grandfather first offered to start me in karting.'

'Yes, your mother was actually the one who helped

me realise that I was being stubborn. Luca has always shown a huge interest in racing, whether he knew you or not. Which…brings me to the next part.'

Astrid turned to their son, beckoning him over with her hand on his elbow. 'Luca asked me something last night, and I told him that I'd like him to ask you himself, if he still wants to.'

Luca's serious green gaze, so like his mother's, flickered briefly up to Apollo's. He shook his head, indicating that he did not wish to repeat his question verbally, so Astrid stood up to her full height.

'He asked me if you are his father. Well, he told me he thinks you are.'

Apollo froze, uncertainty filling him until he took in the calm expression on Astrid's face. This was the next part of her gift, she'd said… Understatement of the century. Emotion clogged his throat as he lowered himself to his knees in front of his young son.

'We wanted to give you some time to get to know me first, but you figured it out all by yourself, huh?' he said softly.

Luca nodded once.

'Your mummy told you that your father lived far away and that he didn't know about you yet, yes?' He extended his hand, waiting a beat and exhaling a relieved breath when Luca placed his hand easily into the centre of his palm. 'I've waited a long time to meet you and I'm very glad that we found each other. I'm very excited to be your *papa*, if you are happy to have me.'

'Papa,' Luca repeated with a curious frown, reaching out his other hand to gently touch the hair on top of Apollo's head. He felt the weight of the small boy's assessment of the tight curls, so like his own, wondering if he had gathered all these little markers of resemblance between them. His son was a perfect mix of them both, but the shrewdness and *knowing* there in his beautiful eyes, so far beyond his seven years, was all Astrid.

And then came the most beautiful birthday gift of all: a smile that spread over his son's face like dawn breaking across the sky after the longest night.

'Mummy and Papa,' Luca said, looking up at his mother.

He heard a sniffle and looked up to find Astrid lightly dabbing at her eyes.

'Yes Luca darling,' she said, taking a seat on the sofa alongside them and placing her hand in Apollo's. 'You have a mummy and a papa.'

CHAPTER TEN

ASTRID SAT ON a recliner on the villa's main veranda and stared out at the moon's reflection over the inky waves in the bay. After almost two weeks on the island, to sit out here and reflect upon another glorious day spent in paradise had become her evening ritual.

Watching Apollo give his son his first karting lesson today had been slightly terrifying for her risk-averse self, to say the least. But seeing Luca's reaction had been… priceless. Almost as monumental as seeing the look of adoration in Apollo's eyes when their son had mastered the first few steps with ease and showed nothing but excitement for the entire afternoon.

Not only that, but Apollo had approached her to try out the sport for herself and see what the fuss was about. She'd refused at first, her entire being balking at the risk of getting into the fast-moving contraptions. But then she'd spied the challenge in Apollo's face and listened to him jokingly call to the other drivers on track that he'd told them so. His open challenge, calling her bluff, had been almost reminiscent of their old flirtation, so she'd found herself wanting to wipe that smile off his face.

She'd grabbed a helmet, squeezed herself into a suit and almost whooped with laughter and satisfaction at the stunned look on his face when she'd walked back out onto the track. She'd been a terrible driver, of course, considering she'd never got a licence, but she'd done it.

After she'd completed her laps at a painful pace, Apollo had come to her, a dark intensity in his eyes which he quickly smoothed away and had begun trying to coach her. She'd laughed, informing him that it was a one-time affair and she would never set foot in one of those death traps again.

He'd informed her that it couldn't be called a death trap when it was only moving at the speed of a crawling toddler. If she'd already begun to suspect that Luca would rail against going home to rainy London before, it certainly would be a battle now. In the end, they'd had to bribe him just to leave the track with the promise of returning soon.

Having been around Apollo's mother and their laid-back extended family over this short break, it was easy to forget that he had been raised in an entirely different world. A world that he had recently returned to, and might be pulled back into even further...depending on what decision he made. She'd watched him slide into one of the larger karts and glide effortlessly around the track—much to the glee of his young audience—but her mind had been elsewhere as questions and worries had flooded in.

And tonight her son had asked his father to put him to bed. Apollo's eyes had met hers with mild panic, in the corridor between their bedrooms, as Luca's small hand had grasped his and pulled him along. If she'd only had a camera to record the sight of one of the world's champion Elite One drivers and biggest sports-fashion icons being completely ruled by a seven-year-old...

What if her son expected this fun and exciting trip with his father to be their new normal? Of course it couldn't be. She had to return to their life in London and Apollo had a whole racing team to run waiting for him. She closed her eyes, feeling the pressure build behind them every time she remembered how many uncertainties still lay ahead for them all outside of this

'You're still awake.'

A warm voice pulled her from her thoughts and she looked up to see Apollo filling up the doorframe. He'd showered; she could tell by the scent of lemon verbena that clouded her nostrils and the few droplets of moisture that glistened in his hair. She realised her jaw had dropped a little and she hastily straightened in her recliner, feeling more like a starstruck fan girl than a colleague and co-parent. But, honestly, the man always looked like a walking advertisement for a designer fragrance!

And she was fast feeling the effect of being subjected to the sight of his perfectly sculpted body as he swam in the pool every day or ran on the beach. Perhaps it was simply because she had neglected her own body's needs for so long, and then given it a taste of pleasure, only to cut herself off again. Had it already been two weeks since she'd been straddling him on that sofa in Venice, riding her way towards release?

'Is everything okay?' Apollo asked, sliding his big body smoothly into the seat opposite. 'You look flushed.'

'Just the wine,' she said lamely, gesturing to her glass and inwardly cursing her own lack of finesse.

He nodded, but seemed strangely on edge as he surveyed her with a sideways glance. 'I'm glad you hadn't gone to sleep yet. I wanted to thank you for today. I know you worry about safety…it can't have been easy.'

'I thought it would be more nerve-wracking, but you're a great teacher. He really loved it out there. I should have known he would; he's your son, after all.'

A boyish smile, so reminiscent of Luca's, transformed Apollo's face. 'He's amazing.'

A comfortable moment of silence fell between them and Astrid felt the strange urge to reach out and touch his hand, needing some point of contact. Which of course was ridiculous, because she had been the one to lay down the rules between them. Why on earth had keeping things platonic seemed like a good idea again?

'You said that taking Luca karting was a gift for me, something to give the man who has everything. I expect you to allow me to reciprocate.'

'That's not necessary.'

'I disagree.' His eyes met hers earnestly. 'When's the last time you did something selfish? Something that was just for you?'

She thought upon his words and how every instance she could think of involved him. Apollo hidden behind a mask, making her giggle and forget her job. Apollo kissing her in the darkness, tempting her with everything she knew she shouldn't take. Then, a lifetime later, straddling him on his sofa and surrendering herself to pleasure…

'I travel first-class by myself for work sometimes,' she said breathlessly, pushing away those memories. 'I buy designer shoes, get my nails done. I don't know what else you expect.'

He tutted, shaking his head. 'I'm not talking about stealing little moments here and there in between your duties to our son or to Falco Roux. I'm talking about switching off completely sometimes and allowing yourself to just…be.'

'I'm not really very good at that.'

'I noticed.' He smiled, a sinful curve of his full lips that made her stomach swirl. 'You deserve to be unashamedly spoiled, Astrid Lewis. I'm asking you to let me.'

His fingertip traced a slow circle upon her skin and she felt her throat turn dry with the immediate effect that tiny touch had on her body. His eyes burned with intensity upon hers as he waited and she felt poised on the edge of a precipice. What on earth was wrong with her? The most beautiful man on the planet was asking permission to spoil her…and she was hesitating!

'I…okay,' she agreed, a strangled sound escaping her throat as his fingertip moved higher up the delicate skin of her wrist. 'What did you have in mind?'

X-rated images immediately filled her imagination, her body heating at the look of pure hunger in his gaze. But to her frustration he removed his hand from hers and placed it back on his knee.

'If I told you, that would ruin the fun.'

'I don't find surprises fun.' She laughed nervously. 'I like a loose plan.'

'You like *control*,' he corrected. 'I plan to show you that giving that up for a little while can be very enjoyable. Do you trust me to care for you, Astrid?'

The urge to lean into him, to let him take over, was so strong. Still, that scared part of her resisted—the part that craved schedules, routine and safety checks to ensure that the rug was never pulled out from beneath her again. Such as the time when she'd gone to her parents with her pregnancy, needing help and reassurance. Instead she'd been turned away and discarded for breaking their rules. So she'd created a brand-new life and rulebook all of her own that no-one could take away.

Apollo wasn't asking her to do that, though, was he? He was offering her a gift, he'd said. Perhaps the greatest gift she could give herself was one last night with him before they returned to reality.

'Yes… I trust you.' She closed her eyes, swaying towards him, only for his lips to tilt and make soft contact with her jaw. He laid a few kisses along it, his breath coming just as hard as hers.

'This actually wasn't part of the plan,' he murmured. 'And I don't think—'

'Shut up and kiss me, Apollo,' she breathed, turning and searching, offering herself to him in a way that would have made her sober self cringe with mortification. She was vaguely aware of his hands smoothing down over her hips, pulling her closer against the very obvious ridge of his erection. She pressed herself against him, glorying in his swift intake of breath. She'd craved his touch for the last two weeks, resisting the urge to break her own vow and go to him. She was so tired of ignoring this pull between them, so tired of worrying about the future. She was just tipsy enough not to care and the realisation made her bold. Then, the infuriating man pulled away. 'Wait… where are you going?'

'You've had a drink…otherwise, believe me, neither of us would be sleeping tonight.' He trailed a finger along her cheek. 'All will be revealed tomorrow. Sweet dreams,' he murmured softly, walking inside and letting the veranda door snick closed behind him.

* * *

The first part of Apollo's surprise turned out to be the arrival of Jem the following morning, much to the excitement of Luca, who immediately began pulling his nanny by the hand and forcing her to take a grand tour of the villa, the pool and his favourite treasure burial spots on the beach.

Apollo had been vague in his instructions: a car would pick Astrid up at noon, and she should pack a change of clothing and a bathing suit. As she retreated to her room to obey his orders, she fretted over whether or not Luca would be upset at her leaving. It had been a long time since she had taken this length of time off work in one go.

Even now, she hadn't been able to avoid the urge to keep checking in on her emails, which evidently Apollo had noticed. Switching off from work usually meant throwing herself into caring for Luca, but with Apollo there to take up half the parenting duties, she'd felt rather…adrift. Perhaps she'd grown used to using busyness and productivity to avoid being left alone with her own feelings. She knew that her team was competent and, and as Tristan had advised her, she was far too close to this particular storm to be of any help. Plus, a large part of her was relieved to be hidden here in Apollo's little slice of paradise, far away from the chaos back home.

She knew that opening herself up to all the commentary and opinions that were likely swarming the media right now would only harm her self-esteem and make it harder for her to return to work when the time came. She would have to brave the fallout eventually, but for now… she would enjoy the reprieve.

It turned out she needn't have worried about Luca's

separation anxiety at all, for her young son only ran to her for a quick hug when she prompted him, before hurriedly running back to continue a game of draughts with his grandmama. Jem had been starstruck by the sight of Leona Hart all morning, much to Astrid's amusement, and the trio had practically shooed her out the door at noon to whatever mystery location to which Apollo had arranged for her to go for the day.

She had thought Apollo would accompany her and had tried not to show her confusion at breakfast when he'd announced that he had a day of meetings planned before a surprise karting lesson for Jem and Luca in the afternoon. But, as she made her way down to the limo, she felt her stomach swoop when he came striding around the far side of the villa, his hair wet from swimming and his shirt open to the waist.

'Good, you haven't left yet.'

'Have you decided to come with me after all?' she said, feeling mildly guilty at the pleasure that thought gave her.

'Luca wouldn't be too happy if I ruined his opportunity to beat Jem on the track.' He smirked. 'Besides, I told you this gift is for you alone, Astrid. Otherwise, it wouldn't be much of a selfless act, would it?'

'It's not *my* birthday.' She chewed her bottom lip, trying to hide her unease.

A warm hand tucked beneath her chin, tipping her face back up to look at him. 'It doesn't have to be an occasion for me to want to spoil you. Today, you're following my orders.'

His husky words made gooseflesh spread along her skin. She inhaled a breath, his scent filling her lungs. 'You sound way too satisfied at that prospect.'

'You have no idea,' he murmured close to her ear. 'You'll be joining me later, for dinner.'

'Just us?'

'Just us,' he confirmed.

Her heart fluttered in her chest. She had always heard that Apollo was a smooth talker with the ladies, but *this*… this felt far more intimate than his playful flirtations of the past. His eyes met hers without hesitation, his hands reaching forward to smooth a path up her bare arms.

'Just to be clear, by "dinner" I mean a proper date.' He leaned forward a bare inch before pulling back. 'You promised me one of those a long time ago. I intend to collect on that debt.'

'As I recall, I only promised you one drink,' she pointed out, feeling the heat of his attention on her like a brand.

'Consider this nearly eight years' interest.' His eyes held a trace of mirth before he seemed to sober. 'Your gift today is given without strings or expectations; I need you to know that. But I'd be lying if I said that my plans were completely innocent.'

'I'd be lying if I said I wasn't hoping they weren't,' she whispered.

His gaze darkened, the pad of his thumb smoothing along the delicate skin of her wrists and making her shiver. No words passed between them, but they didn't need to. The sinful smile that spread across his lips was more than enough to convey exactly what he intended… and she knew without a doubt that this time she would accept. She would turn off her risk-averse brain for one day and accept this gift for what it was. She had spent the past weeks thinking herself into knots, wanting him so badly but not letting herself risk their fragile new co-parenting relationship. She was tired of fighting herself.

'I'll pick you up at five,' he said simply, before taking a full step back and tucking his hands into his pockets, as though willing them to stay where they were. 'I'll be checking in to make sure you're obeying the rules.'

The rules? Before she had a minute to question him on that cryptic statement, her car door was closed and she was whisked away.

Her surprise turned out to be an entire day of treatments in a luxuriously chic eco-spa on the other side of St George. The resort was built in the most beautiful wooden style, nestled in between the natural foliage, and stretched along its very own private beach.

Astrid was greeted by a woman who introduced herself as Apollo's aunt, and pulled into a familiar hug as the woman eagerly gave her a tour of the resort.

'From what I've heard, you two have had a whirlwind romance.' The woman smiled, leading Astrid into a calm treatment room where soft music played and the air smelled like lemons and jasmine.

'We've enjoyed…reconnecting here,' Astrid said, trying to be diplomatic.

'I'm glad he finally has someone sensible to pin him down. His whole family have lived a life of fame and luxury, but all that travelling between homes and hotels… I often wondered how a man could ever learn to be still after a lifetime on the run.'

Astrid didn't know what to say to that, knowing that Apollo still very much planned to live his life of travel and glamour going forward. Nor would she demand he stop. As though sensing her reserve, the older woman set about changing the topic of conversation.

'Has he taken you to the turtle sanctuary yet?'

'Turtle sanctuary?' Astrid asked.

'Oh, it's his pride and joy; he always tries to get back for when the babies hatch and go off at the end of October.'

Astrid pulled out her phone the moment the other woman left the room, intending to fully search this mysterious turtle sanctuary...only to find there was no signal. Not only was there no signal, there was also no Wi-Fi. She paused, remembering the sign she had seen in the reception area: *Rules of your stay: Rest. Reset. Disconnect.*

'Off-grid... really?' she whispered to herself, remembering Apollo's smirk as he'd told her to obey the rules.

She found out exactly what those rules were when her phone was placed into a delicate little box after she was shown to her own private dressing room. She was not simply being offered the opportunity to reset and unwind, she was being *forced* to. Her body felt stiff and tighter than ever as she lay down on the massage table and awaited her first full-body scrub treatment. Once again, she realised how dependent upon technology she'd become as a way of blocking out the maelstrom of her own thoughts. Would it hurt to take some time completely for herself?

The problem was, she was finally alone, and all she could think about was Apollo and how close she'd come to throwing herself at him last night. If she was honest, that was pretty much what she had done, only he'd been a gentleman and walked away. She groaned in embarrassment, burying her face into the towel-covered pillow and trying to ignore the flare of awareness in her body just thinking of the look in his eyes as he'd sent her off today.

The feeling of losing control around Apollo Accardi seemed a constant inevitability. Perhaps she'd been more of a fool to think she could ever stay away from him. Would she regret not allowing herself this time, once they left this beautiful island and returned to reality?

Her mind raced for a while as her body was smeared with a fragrant island-made concoction and her skin was buffed and exfoliated to within an inch of its life. But, as she lowered herself into a warm, fragrant bath to wash off, she found her body following suit.

She listened to the peaceful music playing from the speakers in the ceiling, closing her eyes and allowing her body to sink back into the flotation pool. By the time she was called to her massage appointment, she felt as though her body were made of butter, and her mood was certainly lighter. In fact, as she was served herbal tea on the veranda overlooking the beach, her body lamented the fact that Apollo had sent her here alone and that he hadn't joined her. She leaned back, a low laugh escaping her lips. She was being slowly seduced by a master; there was no mistaking it.

She found a beautiful dress hanging on a rack in her dressing room. A note in Apollo's handwriting informed her to meet him on the beach at sunset. Her body practically vibrated with awareness as she slid the soft, linen fabric over her body. The low cut of the bodice and off-shoulder sleeves meant a bra was not an option. She stared at her reflection in the full-length mirror, her hands tracing how the garment nipped in at her waist and skimmed floatily over her hips and thighs before ending just above the knee. It was completely different to anything she would have chosen for herself, the emerald-green setting off her eyes to perfection.

He'd pretty much promised he'd wait for her to come to him, had he not? She bit her lower lip, wondering what it might be like fully to give in to her fantasies and let Apollo take the lead.

CHAPTER ELEVEN

APOLLO WATCHED ASTRID'S eyes widen as they walked along the streets of St George, now utterly transformed and in full swing for the island's annual Spicemas celebrations. Performers in elaborate costumes bustled past them towards the traditional competitions and parties that filled up most of the week ahead in the capital.

Apollo had barely relaxed since he'd collected Astrid from the spa resort half an hour before. He'd taken one look at her wearing the dress he'd selected and felt his gut tighten with desire. Astrid had begun to look more relaxed in shorts and tank tops running around the villa, but that was nothing compared to the sultry seductress who now walked alongside him.

Her sun-kissed skin seemed to glow under the warmth of the setting sun, and her short brown hair had been left to dry naturally in delicate waves around her face. She wore only the barest hint of pink lipstick on her full lips, a rose-petal colour that matched the sleek spectacles she wore, as well as the perfectly polished pink tips of her fingers and toes.

The urge to call off his plans for a fun evening and simply pull her into his arms was strong, but he resisted. Even now, seeing her obvious pleasure at watching a troupe of soca dancers perform, he spent most of the time looking at her rather than the festivities. He'd never felt so off-balance in pursuing a woman. He didn't want to come all this way only for her to retreat from him once again but, to his surprise, she was already moving towards him. The scent of vanilla, butter and honey enveloped him as Astrid's arms moved around his neck and clung.

Hugging him… She was *hugging* him.

'Thank you,' she said simply, the barest hint of emotion in her voice as she pulled back, a little embarrassed. Not willing to allow her to feel even a second's hesitation at her very welcome embrace, he held onto her wrists, stopping her from retreating from him fully.

'Believe me, this is my pleasure. Look at you…you're rejuvenated.'

'I feel it. I didn't even collect my phone after the spa.'

'Good.' She wouldn't need it, he added mentally, not if the rest of the evening went how he planned.

Perhaps another man might have booked a private restaurant for fine dining, or even a yacht out on the bay. But Apollo knew that, to wow someone with great food in St George, take them to a Spicemas barbecue. The small family-run restaurant had its own private beach, the dining area being rows of picnic tables and grass umbrellas in the open air. Almost every table was filled with local folk and tourists alike, the mood one of lightness and excitement as platters of food were served amidst the string lights and bright carnival decorations.

'Named "Spicemas" after our reputation as the Isle of Spice, the carnival embodies the energy and vibe of

Grenada. It's the ultimate celebration of our people and culture,' he told her.

'I love all of this. The soca and calypso songs, the sweet steelpan music...' She sighed. 'I've travelled the world with Elite One, and I've always loved traditional masquerades and parades, but this is just magical. I'm so glad that Luca has had the chance to experience this part of his family's heritage.'

Apollo placed his hand over hers as she remained rapt, watching the performers finish up a particularly intricate dance number on the small stage. When couples began to move onto the dance floor and join in, he didn't hesitate to pull Astrid to her feet.

'Oh gosh, no. I have two left feet, I—'

'You sound so utterly buttoned up, it's delicious unravelling you.' He twirled her along his arm with ease, sliding them out into the throng of dancers on the sand. He'd removed their shoes at the table, accentuating their height difference. She hadn't been lying: dancing was most certainly not Astrid Lewis's forte, to put it lightly. He laughed as she attempted a weak shimmy to the steelpan music and was rewarded with one of her trademark glares. But, just as quickly as she narrowed those beautiful emerald eyes, her lips widened into a grin and she shimmied with renewed vigour.

'You're jealous of my moves, Accardi!' she exclaimed breathlessly into his ear, her arms flung around his shoulders as she fell against his side. He pulled her close, pressing her chest flush against his torso as the music slowed into a more contemplative rhythm. It wasn't a slow set by any means, but a brief reprieve. They swayed in one another's arms for a long while, until the music sped up again, and he took the opportunity to guide Astrid away from the crowd towards the small pier that led out to a covered gazebo on the water.

'As far as dates go, how am I doing?' he asked, tipping her head back slightly to see her face.

'I wouldn't know,' she said shyly. 'This is the first one I've been asked on.'

'Since Luca?' he asked.

'Yes…but also before.'

Her eyes shone with the reflection of hundreds of string lights around them and he knew she wasn't lying, even as the reality of that statement punched him in the gut. He wanted to know more about her; he wanted to know everything. 'Why?'

'My dad was a small-time politician with lofty dreams, my mum played the role of the perfect wife alongside him. I grew up with very clear rules and expectations.' She shrugged. 'Casual dating was not allowed. I went off to college in London at eighteen, but somehow my first boyfriend was a guy from my home town. We used to eat noodles together in the canteen, if that counts as a date.'

'Was it serious?'

'I had no idea who I was or what I wanted back then. He was pushy and selfish in all aspects of our relationship… Still, I thought it was *so* romantic when he suggested we get engaged after only a year.' She rolled her eyes, forcing a smile that Apollo did not return.

'It didn't last long,' she continued more quietly. 'Not once I found out it was all orchestrated by our fathers to further their political dreams. My father was so angry when I broke it off, he tried to stop me from accepting the internship I'd been offered in Elite One. I had just turned twenty-one, and I wanted to see the world,' she continued, smiling sadly. 'My parents didn't take my rebellion well. But that was nothing compared to how they reacted when I returned six months later and told them I was eight weeks' pregnant and had no idea who the dad was. They urged me to consider my options, and said it would be better to end the pregnancy so that I could focus on my career. But, once I knew I was keeping my baby, they disowned me. They've never even met Luca.'

'I wish I'd found you,' he said. 'I hate that you endured that alone.'

Her eyes shone with emotion for a brief moment, before she turned her face away from him. 'I wish you had too. For Luca and for you.'

'For all of us. I would have done the right thing then, you know. I would have asked you to marry me and made us a family.'

'You don't need to say that. It's in the past.'

'No. Don't hide from me, not here. What happened to us…it's not something either of us caused or can change. But I need you to know that, from now on, you have me. I'm not going anywhere, Astrid.'

His control snapped and he claimed her lips in a kiss filled with all the longing and need her story had unlocked in him. The past was done but the present was right here: she was here in his arms. She reached up on her tiptoes and kissed him back, her lips slow and explorative at first before she leaned in and forced a groan from him. His hands roamed down her back, finding the curve of her bottom and pulling her into where he was hard and aching for her. Apollo drew back with great effort, leaning his forehead against hers.

'I deliberately opted to bring you here, where there were crowds, so that this wouldn't happen… Though, I would be lying if I said I hadn't thought about ways to seduce you back into my bed from the moment we arrived here and you laid down your gauntlet.'

'Apollo…'

He raised her hand, pressing it against his lips, needing to show her that what they had could be more than just stolen kisses or one night of passion. *They* could be more. But he still wasn't sure that wouldn't make her run.

'I know what I want, Astrid. I know that I can give *you* what you need. I can't stop thinking about you, looking at you, wanting you…' He ran his hands upwards along the smooth skin of her shoulders before cupping her jaw delicately. Another man might think of the way she looked up at him through her lashes as shyness. But his Astrid was not shy. She was cautious, yes, and perhaps a little prim at times, but she would not shy away from him. Not here. Not tonight.

As if she heard his thoughts and was determined to prove him right, she stepped closer, pressing her ample chest against him and letting out the most delicious little sigh at the contact.

'Perhaps giving this speech before I got you to our next destination was premature.' He laughed. 'This was not my plan.'

'Plans are overrated, right?' She smiled, her eyes filled with mischief. 'Let's forget the plan, Apollo. You said I should have more fun. Let's just live in the moment.'

'You're sure?' he murmured. 'We can go home if you're worried.'

'And interrupt the sleepover? I'll never hear the end of it.' She paused for a long moment, her eyes searching his. 'Apollo…what if I don't want to go back yet? I want to stretch this one night out a little longer…and just be me. Just be us.'

'One night was never going to be enough. If you haven't figured that out by now, I think I need to try a little harder.'

And then his lips were on hers again, hard and demanding. Her hands touched him now with abandon, her pointed little nails scraping up the back of his neck and sending ribbons of fire down along his nerve endings. This was the Astrid from his memories, the woman who had passionately kissed him in a darkened lift and stolen part of him in the process. Her hands roamed under his shirt, her fingertips caressing his stomach, then moving lower towards his belt.

Her breath caught as he nipped her lower lip with his teeth, capturing her hands above her head. 'Is this not against the rules, Astrid? Trying to undress me in the dark again?'

'I'm thoroughly enjoying being corrupted by your influence.' She smiled wickedly.

'You won't enjoy us being arrested for indecent exposure.' He raised one brow, reaching out to grab her by the hand. 'Come on; I have somewhere I'd like to show you.'

Maybe seduction was part of the plan, he rationalised. He'd meant to wine and dine her, to gradually lead her round to the subject of marriage. Her revelations from her past had given him pause, but they'd helped him understand why she was so focused on avoiding mistakes and conflict. He needed to prove to her that marriage to him would not be a mistake. If she still thought that he simply wanted one night of passion to draw the line under their sexual history, he'd show her why walking away from him was not a possibility.

CHAPTER TWELVE

APOLLO LED HER along a pathway through the foliage and up along a rugged cliff edge, and as they climbed the carved stone steps he pointed to the various sights of St George visible in the distance. He told her how every aspect of the resort had been thought out and planned to keep the natural shape of the island and avoid inundating the landscape with more concrete and glass. She heard her own swift intake of breath when they reached the top step and she caught sight of what he'd told her was one of his favourite places in the whole of Grenada.

His treehouse, as he called it, wasn't quite built up into the trees so much as it had been nestled between them so that it almost blended seamlessly with its surroundings. It was fully fitted out inside, with tiled floors and running water, and all the modern amenities that one might expect of a wealthy man's home. But it was quiet and cut off from the rest of the island in a way that suited the deepest part of him.

'This place is amazing, Apollo.'

'Not here,' he growled, easily lifting her up in his arms. 'Fair warning: when I finally get you into a bed, I don't plan on letting you out of it for a very long time.'

She was vaguely aware of him lowering them both to

the bed, tucking a pillow beneath her head before pulling back. His eyes were dark and attentive as he smoothed a hand along her jaw in that way she liked—the way that made her feel treasured and possessed all at once.

'Please, Apollo,' she urged, reaching for him, but he was already sitting back on his heels, staring down at her.

'I'm going to take my time now, I think,' he said, his voice a husky murmur as he trailed his fingertips down her neck and along the sweetheart neckline of her sundress. 'I finally have you in my bed, right where I want you… I don't want to miss a single second of you losing control for me.'

Oh…he was a dirty talker, alright. The memory of the sinful words he'd rasped in her ear all those years ago came flooding back with full force and she practically whimpered at the need to feel his body against hers. This felt like a punishment and reward all at once, finally having his full attention.

'Have you any idea how long I fantasised about having you like this?' he asked, his eyes still glued to where his fingers slowly peeled back the linen material of her dress from her skin. As the dusky pink of her nipple was revealed to his hungry gaze, he moaned low in his throat. 'Look at that…spread out for me like a treat. This is the only way you should be pleasured, out in the open, where every perfect inch of your skin is on show.'

As if to emphasise that point, he dipped his head and *licked* her. It was possibly the most erotic thing she had ever seen. She couldn't look away as his mouth traced a path lower, his fingers slowly pulling down her clothing until her breasts were exposed to the cool breeze.

'God, you are delicious.'

The heat of his mouth almost enveloped one breast whole, her nipple sliding between his teeth in a way that sent a direct hit of pleasure to her core. She was already damp for him; she had no idea how she might last any longer without bursting into flames entirely.

A row of buttons were all that kept him from seeing her completely bare and she couldn't stop the flash of insecurity, wondering what he would see. Her body had changed a lot with her pregnancy, stretching and growing their child, and bringing her almost to the brink of what she'd thought she was able to do as a human. But, as his hands smoothed down over the softness of her stomach and hips, his lips followed suit, kissing along each thin line, and she felt herself relax into the sensations he invoked.

This man had proved to her over and over again that his attraction was the one thing she did not need to guess at when it came to them being together. The desire that she had felt for him from the moment they'd first met was a kind of deep, primal hunger and awareness, not something ruled by the perfection of his muscles or the stark lines of his perfectly chiselled jaw. So why wouldn't it be the same for him?

'I wish I could have seen you pregnant…growing our child.' He kissed across her skin, his eyes meeting hers. 'You should have been worshipped then, but I'll have to do my best to make up for it now.'

'I'm all for worship…it's been a long time for me.'

'How long?' he asked. 'Wait…you don't have to answer that. It doesn't matter; all that matters to me is that you're here with me now, not how you spent our time apart.'

'I haven't been with anyone else. Not since I fell pregnant.'

Apollo's gaze sharpened upon her, his fingertips tightening at her waist. 'No one?'

She shook her head slowly.

'Why?'

'Many reasons…time and lack of interest. But mainly because the only person I thought about was a man I couldn't find.'

'Astrid…' He tutted softly. 'You're telling me that all this time, you've been completely unsatisfied, untouched? It's a crime. I thought of you, too, almost every time I stepped into that lift, so much that I had to stop going back to that hotel. Flashes of your scent would hit me when I was out in public and I would convince myself that you were somewhere nearby. Desiring you…it drove me mad. I used to take myself in my hand, and try to cling to every second of memory that I could recall. Did you ever think of me, all alone in your bed?'

She knew what he was asking, and she pushed past her own embarrassment, sliding her hands down along her body while his hungry gaze followed the movement 'Yes. I used to touch myself, trying to re-create the way you touched me.'

'Show me.'

She did as she was told, sliding one finger along the moist seam of her sex and circling herself right where it felt best, just as she had done for years all alone, bringing herself to quiet climax to the memory of that one perfect encounter. It wasn't just that time that had fuelled her fantasies, of course; she had a little imagination. She frequently imagined how her mystery lover would come and find her, striding into her bedroom like some kind of white knight and immediately falling to his knees to worship her…not unlike this very moment.

She wouldn't fool herself into thinking he was her saviour or anything of the sort; she did not need saving. But she did need him, at least in this way, and she was pretty sure he needed her too.

She touched herself slowly at first, then began to quicken her pace as her pleasure built. Apollo's eyes darkened and his nostrils flared, his hands sliding from her knee up to her hips and down over her wrist, till his strong fingers covered her own.

'Don't stop, Astrid. Show me how you longed for me; let me see you.'

She realised that he meant her to bring herself to climax in front of him, and the idea of it was so overly shocking she felt her insides coil even tighter as she began to move up against the combined pressure of their hands. 'Apollo…'

'That's it, my name, only mine on your lips while you lose it for me. Let go, let it all go, and show me how perfect you are.'

The way he talked…the way he looked at her…every part of this…seemed to combine into a perfect storm of desire and she knew she was about to do exactly as he said. Her release built slowly at first, with the pressure of his hand throwing off her own usual rhythm, but then she was no longer in control. He was.

She felt the ripples of her release move through her like a wave, washing away every last vestige of doubt that she still possessed about this wild thing between them. Because nothing that felt this good, this *right,* could ever be bad.

As her breathing slowed, and her heartbeat raced, she was aware of Apollo taking her hand in his own. He clasped her fingers, still slick with her own desire, and raised it to his mouth, cleaning away every last drop of her release. She didn't even have the good sense to be embarrassed or shocked; watching him do something so depraved only seemed to stir her desire deeper. Her release had simply loosened something within her rather than completely assuaging it, and she wanted more, so much more.

But, first, she wanted to see him.

Feeling emboldened, she found the strength to raise herself up from the bed and pushed him down until he lay on his back looking up at her. He didn't need to, of course; he outweighed her in size and strength, and could easily have resisted, which somehow made his compliance all the more meaningful.

She took a moment simply to explore his body with her hands as he had done with her, following the ink of the tattoos that covered the wide expanse of his chest and shoulders; feeling the coarse hair there, which she was very grateful he hadn't waxed away. The power in his frame was evident in the bulge of muscle on his shoulders, his pecs and lower, to his abdomen, which seemed to tighten at her touch. She had unbuttoned his shirt, but his jeans still remained, although they were visibly straining at the zip.

'I want to see you too,' she said boldly. Taking her time, popping open the top button and sliding the zip down, he easily sprang free from the restrictive material of his underwear. Her breath caught as she took a moment simply to stare at the beautiful, heavy length of him.

This part of him had been inside her before, but she had never seen it. So she took her time, gliding her hands over the silky, hot length of him and feeling where he was slick with the evidence of his desire for her and the effect she'd had on him. She leaned forward, pressing a kiss on the side, meeting his eyes as she slid her tongue from root to tip and tasted a drop.

'*Dio*, Astrid, again.'

Hearing his guttural groan in Italian spurred her on, and she obeyed, sliding her tongue along the length of him once more before completely enveloping him in her mouth. She wasn't practised in this, as Ian hadn't been keen, but she had read how to do it in books often enough. She had always had a very healthy sexual appetite, despite having chosen to remain celibate since Luca's conception.

'I've always been a fan of learning and practising myself.' He made an attempt at humour, which turned into a shout when her mouth fully enveloped him. She was not feeling shy now, no; she was feeling hungry, famished, from the way he had described himself, and she was determined to get him there just as he had done for her. However, she had barely managed more than three thrusts of him deep into her mouth before his hands were in her hair, pulling her away.

'Not good?' she asked.

'Too good, that's the problem.' He exhaled heavily. 'As much as I would love you to witness the conclusion of where five more seconds of that would go, there's something I need far more, something I've not been able to stop thinking about for a very long time.'

Apollo moved over her with surprisingly feline grace for a man of his size, his hands rough on her skin as he spread her thighs and took a moment to roll protection down over himself. She watched his every move, hungry to take in the sight of him, both of them flushed and feverish in their need for one another.

It had been like that the first time, too, she remembered. His hands had been everywhere in the darkness as they'd explored one another, then there had been a moment of calm as he'd shifted over her and rested the hard tip of his erection against her entrance. It had been another time, in another life, and yet she felt the echo of *back then* merge with *right now* as she opened her eyes and watched him slowly slide forward, filling her.

The sensation was like a huge relief, as though her body had been aching for him all this time, just waiting for him to be inside her once again. He fit her perfectly, his girth stretching her to perfection and touching the most sensitive parts deep inside that she could never quite seem to find herself.

'You feel like heaven,' he said, sliding out a few inches then pushing back deeper again. Astrid inhaled a sharp breath, not realising there had been more to go. There was so much of him! And yet it was just the right amount. The sense of being overwhelmed she felt had nothing to do with his impressive size and everything to do with the scale of what making love with him was unlocking within her.

'Do you see how this could be between us?' he murmured between thrusts, his mouth devouring hers. 'One night could never be enough. Tell me you want more, Astrid, and I'll give it to you. I'll give you everything.'

She paused at the intensity in his voice, her mind fuzzy with pleasure. His words were just passion, surely? This night had to be enough; they both had very different lives to return to and a co-parenting agreement to set in place. Still, she found herself giving into that fantasy for a moment—of Apollo wanting all of her. Of him being hers.

'I want it, Apollo,' she whispered, her eyes meeting his.

He growled his satisfaction at her words, eyes closing as he began to move more forcefully. She clung to his shoulders, feeling a lump build in her throat just as the pleasure built deep within her core. With every stroke of his body, every murmur of pleasure and encouragement that escaped his lips, she was closer to losing it. He reached down, adding a finger to her clitoris, and she was instantly done for.

The intensity was more than she could withstand, and she heard herself cry out as a second orgasm built and crested within her; still, he didn't give up nor did he slow down. He moved harder against her, seeking his own pleasure this time, and she urged him on, needing him to lose it too.

She needed to know she wasn't alone in this, that she wasn't just scratching an itch and giving in to the desire between them. This wasn't a surrender, or a moment of weakness. This was something more.

Apollo slowed his movements ever so slightly, his body still gripped inside her heat. His thumb brushed over her cheekbone and he paused, feeling the evidence of her tears. She stiffened, pulling her face away, hiding from him.

'Sorry, I—'

'Don't,' he said sternly, leaning down to kiss away the rest of the moisture. 'Don't dare apologise for showing me how you feel, how this affects you. I feel it too.'

'Don't stop, Apollo.' She breathed the words, gasping as he moved inside her again, and he felt her delicious heat clench around him like a vice.

'Never, *amore*. Never.' He leaned down, resting his forehead against hers, whispering the words like a vow as he restarted his rhythm. He rocked into her slowly at first, trying to draw out the pleasure even longer. But, God help him, she was perfect, and *this* was perfect. His heartrate soared, his chest tightening with the effort of harnessing his own control.

Never in his adult life had he been in danger of losing control to an immediate release this way. Never had he felt this kind of clawing need for *more*, to feel every inch of the woman beneath him. He'd always used protection, and it had never bothered him, but right now he had to stop the image of losing himself bare in her heat, with no barrier between them.

The brief thought of doing just that, of one day deliberately getting Astrid pregnant again, sent him fully past the point of control. His hips took on a more brutal rhythm, working harder and deeper into her, until he was crying his own release up to the sky above.

Afterwards, he took care not to completely fall against her, taking a moment to dispose of their protection safely before tucking her body into his embrace and holding her close as they both recovered. But the effect of his fantasy lingered, burned into his mind like a brand. He knew that, for now, he wanted them to spend time getting to know one another again without the risk of another unexpected blessing.

'Are you okay?' Astrid whispered against his skin, jolting him from his silent brooding.

'I'm more than okay.' Apollo attempted a laugh. 'I'm trying to think of something romantic to say, but you've pretty much short-circuited my brain.'

'You don't have to say anything; we can just enjoy this moment of paradise for what it is,' she said, smoothing the hair back from her face. 'I'm okay with it.'

'I told you, I want more than one night and I meant it,' he said softly. 'A lot more.'

Her mouth thinned into a line, her brow furrowing. 'I know it will be awkward when it's over, Apollo. Not to mention the idea of watching you move on with your fast-paced racing-driver life, while *my* life will most likely stay exactly the same.'

'What if I don't want to move on?'

'What do you mean?' She frowned, confusion making a little line between her brows. 'Your idea of fun is jumping out of a plane. Mine is spreadsheets and rage-cleaning.'

'Opposites attract… I think that's quite evident.' He smirked.

'I'm not saying you're some kind of hopeless playboy,' she said quickly. 'I'm just a realist. You've carved out your perfect life, one that you've worked incredibly hard for, and I've done the same. I don't need you to force this to be more; can't it just be…this?'

Apollo reached down to the trousers he'd hastily discarded before their love-making, and for a moment she worried he was leaving, but instead he seemed to be searching for something in the pockets. He turned back to face her, raised up on one arm now so that he looked down at her in the soft light.

'You said you don't need more…but you've become a pro at denying your needs for a very long time. Quite simply, I disagree.' He leaned down, laying a playful kiss on her lips.

'You disagree?' she repeated, mildly incredulous and unnerved by the calm intent in his gaze as he pulled away and moved to kneel at the end of the bed.

'I'm not forcing anything, Astrid. I'm more relaxed and sure than I've ever been about the future that I want; these past two weeks have shown me that. And I've never been a patient man…'

His eyes met hers in the soft lamp light, his fingers grasping her left hand firmly as he opened his hand, revealing a small hexagon-shaped velvet box in the centre.

'What are you…? Is that what I think it is?'

'Hear me out before you freak out, okay?' Apollo's lips curved into a soft, teasing smile, even though she was pretty sure she'd seen his hand shake slightly as he dropped to one knee on the floor beside the bed.

CHAPTER THIRTEEN

ASTRID STARED WITH shock at the small velvet box, taking a panicked step backwards as Apollo opened it to reveal a ring…a ridiculously *large* and expensive-looking ring.

'Astrid Lewis…you disappeared from my life nearly eight years ago and came back into it with the most amazing gift.' His voice was low and gravelly as his gaze met hers. 'I don't want to wait another second without you by my side. Will you marry me?'

Her eyes flickered from the glittering cluster of diamonds to Apollo's expectant face and for a moment she wondered if maybe she had fallen and hit her head on a rock on the climb up here earlier…if perhaps everything about the past couple of hours had been a dream. She tried to speak and failed, fear and emotion clogging her throat.

'I picked this up last week. I've been waiting for the right moment to give it to you.' A frown marred his brow and he held the box up closer for her perusal. 'I chose emeralds…but, if you'd prefer something else, we can change it.'

'No, it's beautiful… I just…' Astrid swallowed hard. 'I need a moment.'

She didn't know what to say. Her chest tightened as she turned her face away from him, trying to regain some kind of composure. Her treacherous mind showed her a movie reel of another moment in her life—another proposal she'd initially been excited about, only to find out it was built upon a foundation of convenience and expectations.

This was not the same as it had been with Ian, she told herself, and yet…she couldn't shake the sense of nausea in her stomach as the anxiety took hold.

'Are you okay?'

'Am *I* okay?' She half-laughed, forcing the words past the lump in her throat. 'Apollo…you've just asked me to marry you after one date.'

'It might have been our first official date, several years late, but I'll take you on a million more to make up for the wait. We haven't done things the conventional way so far; why start now?' He took her hands, a deep line furrowing his brow. 'Look, I understand that perhaps it's a little fast—'

'A *little*?' Astrid choked on a horrified laugh as she realised this was really happening. He was completely serious, and he was looking at her with such intensity it made her stomach flip. She made to turn away, only for him to hold her tight, caging both her hands against his chest.

'Would you expect anything less from me?' He flashed one of his trademark dimples and Astrid fought the urge to smack it away. She stood up from the bed, wrapping a sheet around her body in lieu of her dress, which she was pretty sure Apollo had strewn along the stairs behind them after peeling it from her body in one smooth move. But it wasn't just the absence of clothing that made her feel bared and raw.

She felt…adrift. The mindless fog of their love-making had lifted the moment he'd dropped to one knee and asked her to marry him and from the way he looked at her so expectantly, as if she was the one acting strangely by not throwing herself into his arms. They didn't know one other, not the way that a couple entering into marriage should. He was a notorious bachelor who never intended to settle down. She should know; she'd been the one who wrote his media scripts. Unless…

'Are you thinking that an engagement would be a great distraction for the media? Because I think a sudden union between us would have the opposite effect, Apollo.'

'You think I'm considering the media in all this?'

'It's not the worst idea. It's utterly ridiculous and unnecessary but I can see why you would…' He stepped in front of her, barring her from moving any further.

'Whatever whirring of possibilities is going through that beautiful mind of yours…stop. I want to marry you, Astrid. I want a wedding, not fake an engagement to improve the optics.'

'Why?' she asked softly. 'Why not ask me to date you, to try things out? We're already in the eye of a media whirlwind; flying home and immediately planning a wedding will seem far too convenient.'

'What's wrong with convenience?' he asked.

And there it was. Astrid closed her eyes, trying not to be surprised that he wasn't suddenly overcome with romantic love and the need to have her as his wife. This was about tidying up their situation in a quick fashion—a convenient marriage.

'We have years of lost time to make up for and we already know we're exceptionally compatible. Why should we wait for some arbitrary length of time before making this official?'

'Official,' she repeated blankly. 'Tell me that this proposal has nothing to do with your need to claim your son quickly and efficiently. That it has nothing to do with your philanthropic playboy reputation currently being torn apart in the media.'

Tell me that you want me, she silently pleaded. Her breath caught painfully in her throat as Apollo's brow furrowed, the ring in his hand glittering between them like a lit fuse.

His dark eyes narrowed. 'We both know that our situation is unusual and doesn't follow any of the regular rules you might have laid out in your orderly life plans. We've been put in a pressure cooker, Astrid. And you know what? It was exactly what I needed.'

She balked but he didn't notice, so intent was he on persuading her.

'Can't you see how good we would be together? All three of us, living under one roof? I want us to be a family.'

'We *are* a family. Luca is already your son,' she said, her voice taking on a higher pitch. 'I don't see why we need to be married in order for you to cement that fact. This…us…it was only ever meant to be just one night.'

He stared at her long and hard, his brow furrowed with the effort of not saying whatever he so clearly wished to. It was as though he were carved from granite, his jaw like steel as he turned to gaze out of the windows into the inky night beyond.

'Apollo… I know this seems simple to you. But to me, marriage has to be about more than just appearances. I don't care what the public think of me, of how we came to have a child together. I spent long enough struggling with the shame my parents put on me as a single mother and recovering from their disownment of me; I can handle a little gossip.'

His gaze softened at the mention of her lack of family, of the mother and father who had tried to force her to abort her son to protect their fragile, small-town reputation. She had survived the worst kind of abandonment and come out stronger; she didn't need to prove her son's legitimacy to anyone, not even to Apollo.

'I'm sorry, I can't marry you,' she said with finality.

Apollo was silent on their journey back to the house, the roads empty as dawn broke over the island. She didn't argue when he said he'd like to take Luca down to the beach without her, giving Jem the day off. Astrid wandered around the empty house for most of the day, her overactive mind not quelled even by taking a long swim in the pool. Not even the entire tub of ice-cream she ate for dinner satisfied her as she paced the veranda, scanning the beach and road for signs of their return.

It was late evening when she realised she'd left her phone on silent from the day before and had multiple missed calls and voicemails from Apollo. He'd texted first to ask if she was having a nice day, then a second text asking if she'd seen the first one. Then he'd left a voicemail to say that they'd be eating dinner at Leona's if she wanted to join them. Then another text just with a question mark. A few moments ago he'd called and left a voicemail to say he was on his way home and Luca was already asleep.

She sat heavily into a recliner that overlooked the bay, the orange and pink sunset mocking her with its romantic beauty. Was this how life would be, once they returned to normality—Apollo taking his own time away with their son, leaving her alone to wonder where they were and wishing she was part of it, wishing they were all together?

She closed her eyes against the burst of emotion she felt rise within her. How could she have grown so used to Apollo being part of their little family unit after so short a time together? How could she walk away from that?

She wrapped a linen throw blanket around herself and let the tears come, her longing and uncertainty pouring down her cheeks as the evening sun began to wane. She didn't even notice Apollo's arrival until she heard her name on his lips and smelled the warm scent of his cologne on the breeze. She opened her eyes as he came to kneel in front of her, his strong hands cupping her cheeks and wiping at the wetness he found there.

'You didn't answer my calls,' he said, worry marring his brow. 'What happened?'

'I missed them, because I was so busy missing you,' she said simply, too tired and too raw to say anything else.

'I missed you too so much.' He leaned in as though to kiss her, then paused, his eyes meeting hers. 'I messed up last night. It was too much, too soon. But, if you think my proposal was just about duty or tradition…you're wrong.'

Astrid took a deep breath to try and calm the frantic beating of her own heart. 'I can see how it seemed logical.'

Strong arms bracketed her against the back of the recliner. She looked up, her breath catching at the sheer intensity in Apollo's gaze.

'Logical?' he demanded. 'There has never been anything logical about the way I feel about you. To call it compatibility or chemistry is nowhere near enough.'

'Apollo…' She shook her head sadly, staring down at her lap to avoid the heat in his gaze and how that instantly made her want to forget every argument she'd mustered. 'We can't base an entire marriage on great sex.'

'Do you have any idea how often I thought of you in the years that we were lost to one another?' He tipped her chin up, forcing her to meet his gaze again. 'In Lake Como, when I first realised your identity, I hoped for just one more night to be free of my obsession with you. After finding out about our son, I tried to think clearly, to keep you at a distance. I thought I could, that maybe it would be better if we remained platonic co-parents.'

She bit her lower lip, remembering how simple that had seemed and how sure she'd been. She watched as Apollo shook his head, tutting softly.

'My parents were romantics—a whirlwind love match with nothing else in common to hold them together when times were tough. Living through their turbulent ups and downs is what made me swear I would never marry or have children, Astrid. I swore that I would never put a child at the mercy of fleeting and fragile adult emotions. What we could have…would be built on something so much stronger—our love for Luca, our commitment to building a family after our time apart. I know you want it, too.'

'I'm afraid to want it,' she said honestly. 'I'm afraid it won't be enough.'

'It's not just that we have great sex. It's your sexy supreme competence. You make parenting Luca look easy and you never make me feel less for having missed so much of his early years. We enjoy one another, we respect one another. You remind me to enjoy the smallest moments, and I spur you to live a little louder. It's the kind of balance I never thought I could have for myself. Take a chance on this. Be a little impulsive with me.'

'Dancing barefoot on the sand, going kart racing, spending the night together here in a treehouse…those things are what most people would describe as being a little impulsive, Apollo. Marriage is a long-term commitment. I'm not religious, but I believe that making vows means something,' she said gently.

'You believe that I would break my vows?' he asked incredulously. '*Dio,* I've barely looked at another woman since I walked into your office last year. I've wanted you since the first time you looked at me over those delicious spectacles and read me your rulebook.'

She was stunned silent at his admission, at the honesty in his eyes as he told her he hadn't slept with anyone in the past year. It was madness, all of this was utter madness, yet she felt a tiny flicker of hope within her grow.

'Maybe it's twisted, how much I savour pushing you to break your rules. And knowing that…maybe…you like breaking them just as much, don't you?'

'Yes.' She kissed him then, her mouth greedy on his, her hands hungrily seeking the heat of his skin beneath his shirt. But he wasn't done; of course he wouldn't let her off so easily, not until he'd said his fill. He held her wrists pinned in his hands, breaking his mouth away from hers and smirking as she made an angry little sound in her throat.

'You want to know what I think? I think that, even if I'd waited years to ask you, you would still be scared to commit to marrying me. You would still hold yourself back, just in case.' He leaned in, running small kisses down her neck. 'Remember what you told me? In our business, every second counts. Strike while the scandal is hot, baby, and take control of the narrative with me.'

Despite her fraught emotions, a stunned laugh escaped her lips. 'Are you seriously using my own PR tactics to convince me to marry you right now?'

'I'm an Accardi, utterly ruthless when it comes to getting what I want.' His voice was a sensual growl, his dark eyes glittering with intent. 'And I want *you*, Astrid Lewis. Make no mistake about that. I want you in *my* bed and no one else's; my ring on your finger. I want our son running in to wake us up every morning. I want there to be an *us*. A team of our own.'

She closed her eyes at his words, at how badly she wanted it too. She'd spent so long being strong, proving that she could do everything alone. She knew that they could make things work separately, that everything she'd said to him when she'd rejected his proposal was true.

But she also knew that last night she'd been afraid. Afraid of how he made her feel. Afraid of how much he made her want him. Apollo wasn't just offering her a cold business marriage. They would share a bed and a life, they would be partners—but she would never have his heart. He was offering as much of himself as he was prepared to give…and maybe she was the unrealistic one for craving more.

For their son, she knew that having a clear label on their relationship would actually be the strongest way to present themselves as a pair. The same was true for quieting the media, too. He'd seemingly thought of all of these answers long before she had, and he had come to one simple conclusion: marriage made sense.

His had not been a proposal made with empty promises of sweeping romance or adoring love; it had been one filled with honesty, thoughtfulness and dreams for their future. It was steady and scary and maybe even a little exciting: all the emotions that Apollo made her feel whenever he looked at her.

She met his patient gaze, realising that she wanted this. She wanted him. She wanted their wild, scandalous headline-worthy reunion simply to be the prelude to their happily-ever-after, even if that wouldn't include love. It would be better than love, because it would be real.

'Ask me again,' she whispered, feeling her entire body shake anew.

He didn't need any further prompting, but he chose to drop on one knee again, his eyes hopeful and earnest upon hers as he spoke. 'Astrid Lewis…will you marry me?'

Astrid closed her eyes for a second.

'Yes,' she said breathlessly. 'Yes, I'll marry you.'

CHAPTER FOURTEEN

ASTRID AWOKE TO sunlight on her face and an unfamiliar weight draped across her midriff. The ache in her muscles was a pleasant throb as she slid out of bed, careful not to wake the very virile man spread out on his stomach alongside her.

The ring on her left hand sparkled in the dawn light as she stood in the open doorway of the treehouse and stared out at the beauty of the ocean beyond. The decision to return and spend another romantic night here had been taken out of their hands once Leona and Jem had spied the massive ring on her finger at breakfast that morning.

Something about the silence and the earthy scents in the air had called to her so much more than Apollo's suggestions of a luxury resort or a night on one of his yachts to celebrate their engagement. She didn't need all the frills his wild billionaire life could offer but she knew that, when she eventually became his wife, she wouldn't be able to refuse them for ever. She would promise to love and cherish him as long as they both lived…even knowing that it was a union born of convenience.

It was fine; it was better than fine. They both knew where they stood and that was a lot healthier than being promised the sun and stars, only to feel devastated when it all came crashing down. They had amazing sexual chemistry and mutual respect, and they had a love for their son and a desire to raise him well. *The rest is just details, right?*

She worried her lower lip, zoning out as the sun rose higher in the sky, creating a watercolour of pinks and oranges on the calm waves. She jumped a little when a throat cleared behind her and she turned to find Apollo wide awake.

'Morning, fiancée,' he said huskily. 'Come back to bed.'

'Fiancée... I don't think I'm used to that yet.' She laughed, sliding back in under the covers and pressing her body tightly against his.

'We have the entire day and night for me to get you used to it,' he said thickly, sliding himself down between her thighs. 'I intend to show you exactly why accepting my proposal was a great decision...starting right now.'

'We are going to have to eat eventually. And maybe take a walk to avoid muscle cramps after last night's efforts.'

'I did miss my training session yesterday.' He feigned thoughtfulness. 'I'll have to be extra-vigorous to really work all my muscle groups.'

'Speaking of training, why did I just get an email from Tristan saying that they look forward to seeing us at the testing track in a few days?'

'I hadn't intended on talking business, not when I have much more interesting plans to debauch you in every position possible.' He sat up against the headboard. 'I haven't said anything to you yet, because it wasn't certain, but my lawyers have been working to break the terms of the will. To allow me to hand the team over to my cousins.' He met Astrid's gaze. 'With everything that happened with my grandfather, Accardi Autosport doesn't hold the best memories for me. I wanted to be able to put my feelings aside, to put things right for the team, but I've been increasingly feeling that my time will be more urgently needed elsewhere—with Luca…and with you.'

'Apollo…that's a very big decision to make.' She sat up straight, her eyes widening. 'Are you sure you can trust your cousins to manage the team as you'd want?'

'I've put measures into place where my cousins will not be able to deal in corrupt practices.' A slow smile curved his lips. 'I emailed Tristan last night to update him. I told him that I'll be finishing the season with Falco Roux as planned.'

'You are?'

'I am.' He laughed as she launched herself into his arms. 'Are you upset that you'll have to keep on top of my scandalous reputation for a bit longer?'

'Of course not. It's just… Apollo, if you are doing this just because of what I said…'

He shook his head, trailing his hand up the soft skin of her wrist to her shoulder, needing to touch her. 'I made a commitment at Falco Roux that I intend to keep. That's just who I am. I think part of the reason why I was tempted to accept the inheritance was because of my own guilt.'

'About your estrangement from your grandfather?'

'Yes, but…not in the way you think.' His jaw seemed to tighten at the memory, 'I had the opportunity to expose him for cheating against Grayson in my final year at Accardi. The season was already over, and I had won the drivers' championship. Then I found out what he'd done. I confronted him, of course, and he threatened to ruin me. That's why I left.' He added softly, 'And, after some investigation, I now know that's why your efforts to find me never got anywhere.'

'Your grandfather knew about me? About Luca?'

'He did. I've been having the lawyers do some targeted digging and discovered that he paid off your private investigator, and had documents prepared to pay you off in the event you got close to finding out my identity. Allegra was the only one he'd told; Enzo had needed her to know in case he ever had to blackmail me. With Enzo dead and leaving me the team, Allegra went straight to the press with the story.'

She felt shocked, then sad, at the lengths Enzo had gone to just to keep them all apart.

He held her close, seemingly determined to get their evening back on track. 'This was meant to be a celebration, Astrid. I will not have it ruined by the ghosts of the past, not when we have an entire future to look forward to.'

'We haven't talked much about that future yet.'

'We will. I have so many things I want to discuss with you…plan with you…but first, I want to make you forget for a little while.'

He kissed another path up her neck and she felt her legs weaken. This man…this persistent, seductive, beguiling man… She knew that they had so many things they needed to discuss and that holding off on them was only delaying the inevitable. But, as his hands began to work their magic, followed by the touch of his lips against her core, she pretty much forgot all thoughts as her mind relaxed into his worship and he made good on his promise.

For the final night of Spicemas in Grenada, a grand drone display was planned in the bay. The pounding music was playing further on down the beach but still Apollo adjusted a set of noise-cancelling headphones over Luca's ears as the first light began to ascend from the collection of boats a short way out in their private bay.

As vibrant bursts of colour fell from the sky all around them, Apollo's lips found hers and Astrid felt the last piece of protection she'd had in place over her heart fall away.

Jem had now gone home to spend the rest of the summer with friends, and prepare for her part-time university course, and Astrid would usually have been run off her feet. But that morning she'd awoken at ten to the sound of splashing in the pool and the smell of freshly made coffee. Her fiancé—she still hadn't got used to that word—was taking her advice seriously and was taking a proactive role in their son's life without fear of rebuttal.

They'd gone back to the karting track almost every day over the past week and Astrid was slightly worried she'd created an obsessive coach in Apollo. Luca, it turned out, had a natural talent for the sport as well as a keen interest. And, with both a father and godfather who were world champions, she rather feared she'd set the tone for the future. She wondered if her over-protectiveness and caution had held her son back from his potential, and if his risk-taking father was exactly what both of them had needed in their lives.

They'd been up early, and spent the day on the beach

with Apollo's family, so it was no surprise to her when Luca's head began to droop on his father's shoulder immediately the drone show stopped. They walked in pleasant silence up the steps to the villa and Astrid whispered goodnight, opting to slip away to her dressing room to begin getting changed for the more grown-up celebration she had planned for the stroke of midnight.

When she emerged a short while later, however, she could hear low voices coming from her son's bedroom and popped her head in the door to see a sight that melted her heart. Apollo lay on the bed, ankles crossed as he talked his way through an album of his racing wins, one of Luca's new favourite pastimes.

'This was the first track where I placed on the podium,' he said softly. 'It's one of the older Italian tracks, and they don't hold premios there any more. And here I am, at my first win in Monaco...that was a really close one. That's where my work is, with a big karting track you can practise on.'

'Papa's track in Monaco,' Luca repeated.

'That's right.' Apollo said. 'You can come and see me race there next weekend when we're back in Monaco. You and Mummy can cheer me on.'

'Luca loves racing.' The little boy nodded.

Apollo smiled and Luca tried to hide a yawn with his little fist, determined to keep watching as his father flipped the pages to show him the milestones he'd worked so hard for. But all Astrid could hear was the pounding of her own heart as she processed the meaning behind Apollo's words. They hadn't yet discussed any long-term plans for their return. To take the rest of their vacation as a chance to be together away from the various pressures that awaited them once they returned had almost been an unspoken agreement between them.

'Luca loves Papa,' the little boy whispered, one small hand reaching up to cradle his father's cheek for the briefest second, his eyes still focused on the photo album.

Astrid felt her chest constrict as she inhaled a soft breath. Apollo's eyes locked on hers in the low light, his look of shock and emotion equalling her own.

'Papa loves Luca too,' he replied, emotion thickening each syllable. 'So, so much.'

Her son's eyes closed at the words, sleep finally claiming him even as his small hands still held a firm grip on the book of racing lore.

Astrid felt the tears escape her eyelids then, the emotion of the moment all too much for her as she backed away and moved slowly down to the living room with what felt like her entire heart in her throat. Seeing her son bonding with his father was indescribable. It was all she had ever wanted and more…

Of course, Apollo would think nothing of making promises to their son in such a quiet, poignant moment. He wouldn't realise that, to Luca, that was akin to a vow. Of course, Luca would adore the prospect of travelling around the globe with his racing-driver father, to all of the cities and races he had once visited as a toddler.

Her own career had been much easier to juggle back then by having him with her all the time. But he'd struggled with the travel schedules and the crowds, despite loving the cars. She hadn't made the choice to move them permanently to London lightly. Since settling him into school, she had rearranged her life to be more stable, to give him more routine and a better sense of control. And it was working; he was happier, and it had just started feeling easier for them both.

Astrid sighed. Apollo had already missed seven years of Luca's life, so it wasn't entirely unreasonable for him to expect her to change some plans in order for them to be together, really. But would he expect her to uproot their quiet little life and follow him around the globe? How would he react if she said no?

She knew all too well that some people were so focused on their plans and beliefs that they wouldn't even consider bending. An image of her stern father entered her mind on the last day she'd seen him, her mother standing by his side. He hadn't cared that his daughter was a grown adult with agency of her own; he'd rejected her simply because she went against their wishes for the life that *he* believed was right for her. A life in which she'd have quietly ended her pregnancy and never mentioned it again. In which their only daughter hadn't shamed their family with the scandal of single motherhood and recklessness.

But, whereas refusing her parents' wishes had been painful, once she'd made the choice to have her baby she'd distracted herself with her plans to keep them both safe and secure. She'd found a sense of purpose and confidence in building a good life for herself and her son away from her controlling father's influence. Their rejection had been a gift, in a way.

The idea of blending her quiet life with Apollo's superstardom had seemed abstract until now, like something they would get to eventually. Now it felt all too close… as though she was getting ready to give up her hard-won independence the moment they stepped off this island. Or perhaps she already had, when she'd accepted his offer of protection. She closed her eyes, the overwhelming feeling threatening to take her composure completely. Apollo had been clear and honest that he wanted to claim them both as his. That he wanted to make up for lost time and live life together, and he meant sooner rather than later. Seeing how devoted he was to his new family should be a good thing.

Frustration built within her as she pulled her hair away from her face, all plans for her night of seduction forgotten. She was not a meek woman; she had never been the type to change all her plans for anyone, and certainly not a *man*. But Apollo was not just anyone, was he? He was the man she…

She paused, staring at her own reflection as a haunting realisation closed in upon her. There was nothing logical or convenient about the way she felt. She was actually considering walking away from her hard-earned routine and her lovely townhouse, even knowing that, in doing so, she'd be putting Apollo's dreams first, ahead of her own. There was no other explanation: she was falling in love with him. Or maybe she was already there. Maybe she had been there, hovering on the edge of foolish lovesickness, from the moment she'd realised who he was.

Apollo could tell that there was something very wrong with his fiancée when he went in search of her after getting Luca to sleep. She stood on the veranda of the master bedroom, her knuckles white with tension as she stared out at nothing. The night was black and the waves choppy as a storm was due to blow in over the next few days.

'What's wrong?' he asked, willing her to look at him.

She turned, briefly glancing into his eyes before once again looking away with a sigh.

'You can't make promises like that to him, to Luca.'

'I can't make promises to our son?'

'Not when it means changing our plans without consulting me first.' She wrapped her arms around herself. 'You promised him that we would go to Monaco with you.'

'Well, yes. We both agreed that we don't want to live separately, Astrid. I don't plan to waste any more time. I intend to find a way to make that happen.'

'Luca is very happy at his school. Jem will be going to university part-time in September, too, so I had already adjusted my working hours and travel plans to settle Luca back into his routine at home before school starts.' Her lips compressed, and she looked away from him once more. 'But you would know all of that if we'd ever had a conversation about the practicalities of this arrangement before now. Instead, we've been avoiding reality.'

'We've been catching up on lost time. Living in the present.' He sighed. 'When will you realise it's okay to not know every detail all of the time?'

'Even if neither of us have a plan?' she asked, exasperated. 'How exactly do you envision our *future* looking, Apollo?'

'Whatever way it needs to look in order for us to be together.'

'So, if it needs to look like you moving to London, walking your son to school each morning and putting your racing plans on hold?'

'That would be rather extreme, obviously.' He frowned, taking in the tautness of her shoulders and how she stood so rigidly apart from him, in such a contrast to the softness and connection they'd been forging over the past week. 'Your work and mine can be quite compatible. You and Luca also both like to travel. You already work remotely sometimes.'

When she shook her head sadly, he felt irritation flare within. He was missing something, evidently; she was unhappy, and he had the feeling that he had done something gravely wrong to cause it. But he would not apologise for wanting his family to be together, for wanting to find a solution that suited them all.

She opened her mouth to answer, but their silence was intruded upon by a call coming into both their phones at once—

a video-conferencing request from Tristan Falco.

Astrid's eyes met his and the reminder of the reality that awaited them was stark between them.

'Don't answer it,' Apollo said. 'Falco can wait.'

'There might be an emergency,' Astrid said, turning from him and striding into the bedroom as she answered the video call on her device. Apollo stood behind her, seeing Tristan's eyes widen as he took in both of them in their nightwear.

'I haven't interrupted something, have I?'

Tristan had flown back to Monaco already, with Nina, who had already begun her training and testing for the upcoming race weekend. Apollo was supposed to be back training too, but he had decided to wait and fly home in a couple more days. His gym here was enough for him to keep up his routine in the meantime. Ironically, he'd changed every single one of his plans because he'd wanted to spend more time with Luca and Astrid here, in their little bubble.

‘We have a problem,’ Tristan said gravely. ‘Elite One has called a hearing. Your right to race the rest of this season, maybe even permanently, is being called into question.’

‘What?’ Apollo growled, his jaw tight with tension. ‘Who initiated this?’

‘I think you know who,’ Tristan said, his own brows knitted tight with tension. ‘Your cousins don’t want the team on your terms, so they’re trying to force your hand. They’re accusing you of colluding with your grandfather to gain your world title win…eight years ago.’

‘They can’t do that!’ Astrid gasped, her eyes meeting his with horror.

They could. And they would. If his cousins were already trying to acquire the team in such an underhanded way, they would never run the team honestly, even if he put legal restrictions in to try and make them do so. How could he ever have believed they would do the right thing?

‘Legal are looking into it, but it’s looking like, at the very least, the severity of the accusations could prevent you from racing next weekend. At worst, you could be completely banned. Which is exactly what they want,’ Tristan said grimly. ‘We need you back over here.’

Apollo hesitated, the very idea of being banned from the sport he adored almost more than he could take. Walking away on his own terms had been one thing, but being cast out for something he had no part in? Being publicly shamed and having his entire career negated? It was his worst fear come to life.

And, to add to it all, Astrid had just been talking about

how his career would always play centre-stage in their relationship; how she'd planned to return to London to settle Luca back into his school routine before the actual school year commenced. These were things he should have discussed with her before he'd made his promise to bring their son to the race. He would need to be more careful, more considerate, in future, if he ever hoped her fully to trust in him as a partner.

'We'll need to show a united front,' Astrid said, nodding. 'Of course. We'll leave first thing tomorrow.'

Apollo shook his head swiftly to protest, only for his fiancée to place her hand gently on his. He covered her hand with his own, his body growing more tense by the second as she quickly wrapped up the video call.

'I'll be travelling alone, Astrid,' he said, standing up, immediately to pace to the other side of the bedroom in an effort to stay calm. 'I am *not* having you and Luca walking into a media storm like this. Not when I brought you here specifically to avoid him being around that. You don't need to—'

'I do.' Astrid's voice was strong as she stood up and crossed the room to where he stood. 'This will not be the same as what you went through as a boy. We need to get in front of this narrative, and luckily you have the best PR guru in Elite One on your team.'

Apollo pulled Astrid into his arms and breathed in her scent. 'Your support means everything to me in this, I need you to know that,' he murmured.

She inhaled a deep breath, before melting into his embrace. 'I know.'

He heard the odd hesitation in her tone and fought the urge to question the taut smile on her lips. Instead, he kissed her with every ounce of passion and gratitude that he possessed. It was a kiss filled with need, and soon he was tumbling her down onto their bed and growling his pleasure as she urged him inside her perfect body. There was no time to roll on protection, no time to think or talk, only to feel. By the time he realised his error and spoke it aloud, Astrid's eyes were glassy with the onset of her own release.

'Don't stop, please.'

'Are you sure? I haven't…' His breath heaved as he forced himself to hold still, though it took every inch of control he did not have.

'This time of the month should be safe,' she said, her voice husky as she wrapped her legs around his hips and pulled him deeper. 'But if you don't want to…'

'Is it wrong that I would still want to even if it wasn't a safe time?' he asked, sliding back inside her slowly. 'Is it wrong that I've thought about filling you more times than I can count? You'd ask me and I'd make sure I didn't stop till I got you pregnant with another child. I'd make damned sure, baby.'

'Apollo!' she gasped, her eyes sliding shut with pleasure.

She clearly liked his dirty talk. This was his fantasy come to life, and he fought not to spill inside her that very second. Sex with Astrid had been utter perfection already, but this—feeling her around him for the first time without any barrier; knowing that she wanted this, wanted him, with nothing between them —was beyond heaven. There was nothing tender or romantic about the way he thrust into her heat, and he felt the feverish urgency building in her just as he could feel it tingling along his spine.

His release was so intense that he leaned down, sinking his teeth into her shoulder. Astrid cried out at the feeling, then immediately lost it, her body gripping and shuddering around his length and tipping over the precipice along with him. He focused on feeling every inch of her tightening around him as he filled her, claiming her body as deeply and hard as he could. Showing her that this was where she belonged, here in his arms.

Fierce possession filled him as she nuzzled deeper into his embrace and he pushed away the faint edges of doubt that whispered he was on borrowed time. He kissed her temple and made a silent vow that he would do everything within his power to make this work.

CHAPTER FIFTEEN

THEY DECIDED AGAINST taking Luca back to London, calling Jem to ask if she'd consider ending her holiday early. She readily agreed, happy to join them all in Monte Carlo and keep the little boy busy and safely away from prying eyes. The press here was usually a little less intense than that in England, being more used to wealthy people roaming its streets. But, from the moment Apollo's jet touched down, they were inundated with photographers, journalists' requests and Elite One fans shouting both cheers and accusations.

Apollo was immediately called into meetings with his lawyers to prepare, while Astrid gathered her own war effort and prepared to battle for their public image. By the time they tucked Luca in and both fell into their own bed that night, Astrid had no energy left to do more than fall asleep in his arms. When she awoke the next morning, Apollo had already got up to eat breakfast with Luca, before heading off for a day of training and more meetings.

Not that Astrid was any less snowed under with meetings and emails, but the reminder that he was also preparing for the upcoming racing weekend had caught her off-guard. As she showered and dressed casually to work from her laptop for the day, she couldn't shake that vague cloud of unease. She'd always been nervous watching Grayson head out on the track, especially in rough weather or after any scrapes or incidents. The life of an Elite One racing driver was fast-paced and unpredictable.

Roux Racing had been one of the oldest and most revered Monaco racing companies and, even after the swift rebrand by Tristan Falco in recent years to Falco Roux—following the Roux family's former scandals—their fans were still intensely passionate. They had been initially lukewarm in accepting the grandson of Enzo Accardi as the primary driver the year before, and this latest revelation in the press about Apollo's involvement in race fraud seemed only to solidify those initial suspicions that he was a plant from their biggest rival.

In her line of work, Astrid was used to having to undo difficult narratives and take control of public opinion; it was one of her greatest strengths that she could always seem to find just the right way to swing a story to get them out of hot water. But, no matter what angle she worked with her team over the coming days, she made very little headway. The Falco Roux fans had turned on their star driver and, in her experience, when that happened, it only spelled disaster for the rest of the season.

The meetings at Elite One headquarters were highly publicised, day-long affairs that required all ten team owners to be present and a handful of drivers willing to testify on Apollo's behalf against the historical accusations—including Grayson, who luckily had already returned to Monte Carlo for testing in the Elite E league.

Izzy surprised them with a visit and Astrid felt her throat tighten as the other woman embraced Luca and her in the hallway of Apollo's shiny marble apartment.

'Yikes, you wouldn't want to have a problem with mirrors around here.' Izzy smirked at her blooming reflection, placing her hands on her sizeable baby bump. 'Don't even think about asking me if I'm sure it's not twins; beware, my mood can change at any moment.'

'I'm glad I ordered in lots of pizza and *gelato*, then,' Astrid laughed.

Izzy's eyes turned cartoon-wide. 'Oh, how I missed you, boss lady.'

The two of them studiously avoided any talk of the crisis at hand as they dined on the large terrace, devouring copious amounts of food while Luca jumped in and out of the pool. Astrid filled Izzy in on every detail of the past month, from realising Apollo was Luca's father to their whirlwind trip to Grenada, finishing with the large ring on her finger.

'It's all so wildly romantic.' Izzy sighed, one hand rubbing her rounded belly. She and Grayson were expecting their second child in a few months. Astrid remembered her own bump and how protective she'd been; how overjoyed she'd felt at the first kicks and every other little milestone, despite the stress of going it alone. She remembered Luca's excitement at finding out Grayson and Izzy were going to have another baby.

Unbidden, Apollo's words on that intense night in Grenada seemed to echo in her mind: *I'd make sure I didn't stop till I got you pregnant.* A shiver coursed through her body, one not entirely made up of anxiety, as she remembered once again their lack of protection that night. It had been so, so reckless and completely unlike her. But then again, when it came to Apollo she had acted out of character. She closed her eyes, remembering the feverish love-making in the lift that had bound their fates for ever. Was she destined forever to lose control of her senses with him? She inhaled a deep breath in an effort to calm the sudden wave of anxiety in her chest.

'Are you okay?'

She looked up to see Izzy eyeing her warily and she quickly changed the subject back to Luca and their beautiful holiday, glad when her friend took the hint and began sharing the latest photographs of summer at their home in Ireland and plans to begin fostering children.

Astrid followed the conversation, genuinely interested in catching up with her dear friend, but at the same time doing mental calculations. She'd been in the very last few days of her menstrual cycle that night in Grenada when Apollo had not used protection, which was the main reason she'd felt safe risking it. She was due today and had always been right on time…with one Luca-shaped exception.

Once she'd hugged Izzy goodbye, she quickly went about procuring a test, knowing that there was a possibility, however slim, that perhaps she and Apollo had conceived a child. She stood in the opulently decorated bathroom and stared down at the window in the digital test result, the blinking cursor taunting her. Another unexpected pregnancy, even if they were engaged to be married, was the last thing that either of them needed right now. But it seemed that, the more boundaries she tried to put in place with Apollo, the more she just ended up breaking them all by herself.

Her insides shook as she stared down at the tiny screen that would decide her fate. Impatience and fear warred with a flicker of…excitement?

A baby would be loved and adored by both of them. But it would only be one of them whose career plans would be changed completely when things were already so uncertain and rocky. By the time the test screen stopped blinking and showed the result, she felt as if she'd already played out every possible scenario in her mind.

Seeing the stark *not pregnant* was almost like a loss, however momentary. It made her feel strange…off-balance and silly. The realisation that she'd been slowly sleepwalking away from the peaceful life she'd built was an unnerving one. Apollo had said they were on a timeline of their own, but she had to remind herself that control and planning were important to her for a reason, and it was important to Luca too. She needed to think things through before diving in—she needed to feel safe and heard—and those needs were valid.

In fact they were more than valid: they were completely necessary if she and Apollo had any hope of making this relationship work.

Apollo already regretted agreeing to go out for dinner with Grayson Koh, even knowing that his support was important to their PR campaign. After another full day away from Astrid, his temper was on a razor's edge, and his old rival's easy relationship with Astrid was more irritating than ever. Even seated next to his wife, Grayson continued to smile and bring up old jokes at which the women gleefully laughed. Apollo fought the urge to bat the handsome Singaporean away.

His every move was being more heavily scrutinised and photographed than ever, likely adding to his crankiness. Not to mention that he'd barely had a moment alone with his fiancée in days. Holding her sleeping body at night was the most he'd managed with their busy schedules. The tension in his body was at its peak, his annoyance undeniable when the other man mentioned his son so familiarly.

'Luca must be starting back at school soon, yes?' Grayson asked, Isabel's and his hands intertwined on the top of the dining table in the fancy restaurant.

'In a few days, yes.' Astrid nodded.

'He won't mind not being at home to settle back in after your time away?'

Astrid paused mid-bite of her dessert, pressing her lips together in a look Apollo immediately recognised as guilt.

'With the press going wild, we decided Monaco was safer for him than London, for now. Luca knows we'll be back in time for his first day at school,' he interjected smoothly, pointedly placing his own hand over Astrid's on the table. 'We can enjoy more family time here until then.'

Grayson nodded but Apollo didn't miss the look he sent towards his wife, Izzy. The other woman had been Luca's nanny for a year between his ages of two and three. Suddenly, he felt as though he was missing something crucial that all of them knew. Their flight back to Monaco had been very different from the one to Grenada only a few weeks before. Luca had been overwhelmed at every sound, upset by the change of leaving their little island paradise and his new family.

Astrid had explained that this behaviour was typical for him, that the hardest part was often when the time came to leave. He struggled with the transition from one activity to the next, so the idea of flying to Monaco instead of London to prepare for school again was huge in his tiny world. But Apollo had already thought of a solution to that problem, one that fitted in with his and Astrid's plans to marry as soon as possible. His son shouldn't have to be moved around at all, and he wouldn't be, once Apollo had a chance to reveal his newest purchase to Astrid.

Grayson narrowed his eyes. 'I only ask because I know how hard Astrid worked to settle him into life in London. How well he's responded to his new routine.'

Apollo immediately bristled. 'I don't think how we raise our son is any of your business.'

Astrid turned to Grayson, a flash of alarm marring her brow as she cleared her throat. 'Apologies, the last few weeks have been so tense; we've all had to adapt quite a bit.'

Apollo watched as she pasted on a smile and smoothed over his outburst like the pro that she was, reassuring her friends that all was perfectly well before pivoting the conversation to neutral territory. Tension remained between Grayson and him as they all bid one another goodbye, but Apollo made a point to pull the other man aside and sincerely thank him for his testimony. From what he'd been told, Grayson had been clear that he believed Apollo to be innocent of any wrongdoing, and that he believed Apollo's championship had been won fairly. The Singaporean champion was an Elite One legend in his own right and did not need to take action against an old rival.

The walk back through the photographers' lenses was quick, but he didn't miss how tightly Astrid held onto his hand. When they finally found themselves inside the sleek interior of his car, she sagged back against the head rest with a sigh. 'I should have expected all of this. I'm already exhausted by it.'

'The paparazzi…or being engaged to me?' Apollo asked smoothly, his hands tight upon the wheel and his knuckles white with tension.

'What?' Astrid frowned. 'I meant the cameras, obviously.'

'The attention comes as part of the package, Astrid. Something you knew quite well when you accepted my proposal.'

'I don't understand your mood right now.'

He shook his head, letting out a deep sigh. 'None of this week was part of the plan. I promised to keep you safe from all this nonsense, too, not just Luca.'

Silent tension fell between them, a distance that had been growing from the moment they'd left Grenada. They had shared a bed, but there had been a distinct lack of closeness and a very obvious thread of anxious tension growing from both sides.

He turned to face her, waiting until her eyes met his in the confines of the sleek car interior. She was so damned beautiful. His chest tightened, and he fought the urge to gather her into his arms, but settled for reaching out to slide a hand along her cheek. She moved towards him unbidden, her lips sliding softly against his in a move so right, so perfect, that it felt like coming home.

A deep sigh escaped his lungs and for a moment he allowed himself just to hold her close and feel their breaths mingle softly in unison. When he pulled back, a dazed smile remained on her lips and a healthy blush had replaced the pinched anxious pallor from moments before.

Suddenly, he knew he couldn't wait another moment to show her the surprise he'd been working on all week.

He drove them along the winding streets of Monte Carlo, out towards the coastal road, and he felt sure about his decision to bring Astrid. The past week of meetings and public appearances had been gruelling on them both, and his temperament had gone in a steady decline the more he'd seen her around Grayson Koh.

He wasn't jealous of the other man or worried about Astrid's devotion to her friend. His animosity was entirely down to the fact that seeing him was a reminder of the time he had missed with Luca and Astrid. It was a reminder of the part that Luca's godfather had played in his son's life while he, Luca's actual father, had been nowhere to be found. Luca had more memories of growing up with his mother's friends than he did with his own father.

This was their new beginning, he reminded himself. This was his chance to make everything right and he didn't want to wait a second longer before revealing his plans to his fiancée.

'Where are you taking me?' she asked, a bemused smile on her lips.

'I've been working on a surprise. I was going to wait to show it to you, but I think we both need something to celebrate, don't you?'

They made their way down onto the smaller roads past mansions and hill-top apartment blocks with stunning views of the entire bay. It was an area that most coveted and few could afford, but that was not a problem for Apollo. He clicked a button on the key set in his pocket and a set of electronic gates slid open, slowly revealing a beautiful two-storey villa nestled into the tree line.

'A romantic weekend getaway?' Astrid asked, a mischievous smile on her lips.

'You'll see.'

He parked at the front beside the grand fountain filled with tiny marble cherubs playfully spouting water at one another. He moved round to the other side of the car, helping Astrid out and offering a bow, like a true gentleman, much to her amusement.

'You're being very mysterious, Apollo.' She raised one brow. 'This is not some kind of secret Monte Carlo society filled with debauchery and depravity, is it?'

'Debauchery?' He pulled her close. 'You think I could stand to share you with another person? I could barely stand to have you laughing and joking with my old rival for most of dinner.'

'Grayson has been like an uncle to Luca and only ever a kind friend to me.'

'I know,' Apollo said apologetically. And he did know; he had looked into Grayson's involvement in Luca's early years and found that his rival had been more than kind in stepping in as a godfather, taking Luca round the track and showering him with gifts, as well as making sure that Astrid's career was not impacted too heavily by her pregnancy.

He was seriously indebted to the other man; perhaps that was another reason why his presence at dinner tonight had been so difficult for him. It was something he would work on, this possessive, jealous streak. Perhaps it would calm down once they were all settled and together under one roof again.

Which brought him back to the task at hand. He took another key from his pocket and opened up the front door, guiding Astrid inside the empty hall. There was no furniture in the villa, just grand, empty rooms. It was a blank canvas, a fresh start awaiting her instructions. Awaiting a family to create a home.

'Well, what do you think?'

Astrid frowned, looking around at the well-decorated space. 'It's beautiful… I'm just not quite sure why we're here.'

'We are here because I just bought it,' he said, taking her by the hand and placing the key in the centre of her palm. 'Welcome to our new home.'

CHAPTER SIXTEEN

ASTRID FROZE IN horror at the expectant look on Apollo's face and knew without a doubt that this was not some poor attempt at a practical joke. He had really gone and bought an entire mansion for them.

Her stomach tightened with nausea as she stared around at the cavernous hall with its glass chandeliers and expensive polished marble floors. To anyone else, this might be seen as a romantic gesture of the highest order. But to Astrid…it spelled only disaster. He clearly assumed she would be moving to Monaco, despite her already having told him the importance of her life in London. He wanted Luca and her by his side, cheering him on and travelling around the world with the racing season.

'Apollo, we've talked about this. About you not consulting with me before making decisions. Did you hear me at all?' Astrid turned and frowned. 'You know my home—Luca's home—is in London.'

'For now, perhaps, but you'll both be moving here as soon as arrangements can be made. As I've told you, London is no longer the safest place for either of you.'

'There is no "for now", Apollo. I won't be moving. I won't uproot our son's life and follow your career around the globe just because you're determined to prove you deserved that first world championship win.'

'That's not fair,' he said through gritted teeth. 'I want you both with me, living as a family. This isn't just about the championship.'

'It isn't *not* about it either, though, is it? I've been in this industry a long time, I know the look of a racing driver on a mission. Don't mistake me; I want it for you too. Like I said when you asked me to marry you, we both have very solid plans for our lives. We're both very driven, perhaps too much so. This idea to move us here is just…it's too much.'

'We are engaged to be married.'

'I think we didn't talk through a lot of things that perhaps we should have. And the timing of all of this is difficult, to say the least.'

'As it is I will be video-calling my son from around the world, updating him with emails and selfies several months of the year,' he said darkly. 'Is it wrong for me to want to have us all together when I'm here? Can't you see that I'm doing this for the right reasons?'

'What I see is a man who is determined to live in an ideal world, where he can have everything and give up nothing in return.'

She saw the frown between his eyes and her heart sank, because she knew that to him this was a perfectly rational way forward. But to her it was an echo of the time in her life when she had allowed other people's wishes to come before her own. She was not that timid young woman any more; she was strong, and she had built a life for herself that she treasured and that she had earned. A life that made her happy, and made Luca happy too in its simplicity… Was it so wrong for her to want to protect that, even if it came at the risk of losing the man she loved?

Because she knew now more than ever that she did love Apollo. She loved him enough to want him to win on his terms and be happy in his success, even if that success took him away from her. She closed her eyes, feeling the breeze blow through her hair, and with it came the spicy scent of Apollo's cologne. Losing him again would be painful; she was not silly enough to think that she would ever have made it out of this situation completely unscathed. But she would not regret taking a risk on him, on them. She would not regret being hopeful, even if it all came tumbling around them so soon.

'What exactly are you saying, Astrid…that you don't want to marry me?'

'I don't know. I don't know what the future holds but I know it can't be like this. It can't take me from the career I've built, and Luca from the stability he needs.'

'You would live apart from me, keep my son from the father he's only just met?' Apollo stepped closer. 'Not to mention, we haven't been careful. What if we're already expecting another child?'

'First of all, I never chose to keep Luca from you, and I never would. Secondly, I'm not pregnant. I did a test this morning.' His eyes widened at her words, but she continued, knowing she needed to get this out. 'I won't uproot my son's entire life; I have to put him first. If you get to race, I will try to bring Luca to see you. We will support you, but we can't travel with you around the world, nor will I move him to Monaco on a whim.'

'I won't allow you to walk away from me,' he argued, a panicked look transforming his face as he took hers in his hands. 'You need to understand. Look at all that we could have, if you just—

'No.' Astrid pulled free, taking a few steps back. She needed space between them, she needed to be able to breathe. Apollo took a step towards her and she threw up her hands. 'I need to leave right now. It was a mistake coming here with you. You convinced me to live in the moment long enough, but it's not working. Luca isn't happy out of his routine. I'm a ball of anxiety…and now you're pushing to fully uproot everything I've built.'

'I'm pushing to keep us together. To build a life together.'

'But this is *your* life, Apollo, not ours.' She swallowed past the emotion in her throat. 'Family is about more than living under one roof. Maybe if you could just stop holding onto us so tightly, if you could stop letting your insecurities lead your actions, you'd realise that your son truly loves you—we both do.'

'Astrid…' He swallowed, his eyes wide. 'Let's just take a moment,'

'Waiting won't change anything, Apollo.' She said. 'I wasn't supposed to fall in love with you, but I did. I don't want a convenient marriage, I want a real one.'

She closed her eyes to block out the utterly stricken look on Apollo's face. He looked like a man drowning rather than one who'd just been told his wife-to-be loved him. But, then again, love had never been part of their arrangement. She looked up at him, willing him just to try to open his heart to the possibility of love.

He stepped forward, grasping her hands tightly in his. 'What we have *is* real. It's more than I ever thought I'd be capable of. Please, Astrid…don't walk away from what we have.'

Something deep within her chest shattered at his words, yet she still managed not to crumble. Her head held high, she removed herself from his embrace. 'I think it's best I return to London. Luca needs time to prepare for school and I… I need some time too. I'd appreciate if you didn't make this difficult.'

'If that's what you want, I won't stop you. I won't force you to stay with me, Astrid.' Apollo's hands clenched by his sides. 'I'll ready the jet for the morning.'

During the short drive to the airport the next morning, Astrid agonised over her decision to leave Monaco. Apollo had calmly agreed to ready the jet when she'd asked, but he had barely spoken to her since they'd left the villa the previous evening. She couldn't help but feel a little like that vulnerable girl, punished with silence for going against her parents' wishes.

Dark sunglasses shielded Apollo's eyes from view as he leaned against the door of the chauffeur-driven car. With Luca and Jem already having waved goodbye and gone inside the aircraft, Astrid waited on the steps a moment longer than necessary, hoping that Apollo would say something. Hoping that he would apologise for pushing. Hoping that he would acknowledge her declaration of love. Hoping that he would choose Luca and her over everything else in his world; that he would realise he needed to put them first.

She waited, watching the slow rise and fall of his shoulders as she stood there, one hand braced on the handle of her suitcase for what felt like for ever…until the time came to admit that it was over. Just as she had that night in Venice a lifetime ago, Astrid walked away, leaving him standing there alone.

Apollo didn't know how long he sat waiting after the jet disappeared from view, nor did he know how long he drove around aimlessly along the coastal roads afterwards. Phone calls from the PR team and Tristan Falco lit up the car's dashboard, but he ignored them. He briefly entertained the idea of driving back to Lake Como and sharing a bottle of limoncello with his father, just as Santo had been urging him to.

His father had yet to meet Luca, which he regretted to a certain degree. But Santo was not the kind of influence that Apollo wished his young son to have. He loved his parents, but perhaps his childhood did have a lot to do with why he held on to people as tightly as he did, as Astrid had accused him of doing.

It might explain why he was so guarded, why he expected people to leave him, so that he kept them at a distance. Astrid had said she loved him, but she might as well have thrown a live bomb between them.

He growled, thumping his hand down upon the wheel at the memory of the hurt on her beautiful face as he'd just stood there, stunned. At how he'd willed himself to say something—

anything—to make her stay. With every moment that had passed without him responding to her, he'd felt her slip further from his reach.

But how on earth could he ever risk falling in love when the example he'd been set as a child was all he knew? His only experience of love was the toxic battleground of his parents' marriage. Even his grandfather, the person he'd relied on to comfort him, had ultimately tried to control him for his own purposes.

Apollo's decision to purchase the house had felt right at the time; he'd thought he'd be able to convince Astrid that they could all be happy together in Monaco. Luca could be happy, too; Apollo had already drawn up a handful of excellent schools and shortlisted some local nannies who had experience with autism, in case Jem didn't want to come to Monaco. He hadn't been completely idealistic, as she'd accused him of being.

Still, even as he'd tried to justify his own actions to himself, he knew that he had messed up. He had pushed too hard once again, and this time he had possibly pushed her completely away. They had barely been engaged any time at all, and he had already lost her.

His phone rang as he drove and he hit a button to answer on the speaker.

'I've been trying to contact you all afternoon. Where are you?' Tristan Falco's voice boomed.

'Out,' Apollo snapped.

'I come bearing good news,' the other man announced triumphantly. 'The hearing result is in.'

Apollo paused, opting to take the next turn off the motorway into a sightseeing spot that overlooked the entire bay. He stepped out into the sunshine, switching the call over to his handset.

'Okay, let's hear it, then.'

'You won,' Tristan said. 'We won, more like. The stewards have ruled in favour of scrapping the charges and allowing you to race for the remainder of the season.

Grayson's testimony helped, of course, but mostly it was your lawyers.'

His team had finally revealed the full extent of his grandfather's actions. The press now knew all the details of his 'secret love child' too. Not that he cared what the public thought. If his grandfather hadn't interfered, Luca would never been a damned secret in the first place! Apollo growled, kicking his foot at a nearby tree. His grandfather had a lot to answer for.

'You know, I've been thinking,' Tristan said. 'Accardi Autosport could really benefit from strong leadership right now. Your cousins are clearly not going to comply with any of the rules you put in place to eradicate corruption. Perhaps a tiny part of your grandfather knew that, too—that there was only one honourable Accardi fit to run that team.'

Apollo thought of the man he'd grown up idolising. Could this have been the reason Enzo had asked to speak with him the day he'd died? There was no way he would ever truly know for certain, of course. But he could take control of his bad memories by taking the helm at Accardi and making something good of the connection he'd had with the man who'd helped raise him. Something held very tightly inside him finally relaxed at the thought.

'I'm confused, Falco; are you suggesting that your primary driver and main chance for a win this season abandons you after all?' he teased gruffly.

'Nina is second behind you in points; she has just as good a chance at winning for us if you choose to drop out,' Tristan said with a laugh. 'Plus, we already have a reserve driver ready to go. No one would blame you if you chose to prioritise whatever makes your family life easier.'

Family life.

Apollo closed his eyes and felt the breeze rustle his hair as he thought of his tiny family that was so far away. The family he wasn't even sure he had a right to be part of any more, not since he'd been so utterly selfish and possessive. Had he already ruined everything?

The image of Astrid telling him she loved him with tears in her eyes shamed him anew. He hadn't responded to her declaration, he had frozen like a coward. She'd accused him of trying to have everything and giving nothing in return.

She was right. He had been stubborn and selfish, fearful of having his last chance to prove himself to the world as a racing driver taken away from him. But, really, had he ever truly needed a chance to prove himself? He had done it eight years ago. His reputation had been cleared, and it had been ruled that he'd had no part in any of the dealings his grandfather had engaged in. His lead that season had been so far ahead of the driver in second place that there'd been no real chance that he could have ever caught up, anyway. Apollo had deserved the win.

But even if he hadn't, even if he'd been banned from the sport today and his racing career had been completely taken away from him, he realised that nothing could make him feel the same amount of pain and devastation as the thought of losing Astrid. At the thought of losing what they'd begun to build together and his connection with his little boy.

He only half-listened to Tristan describe the various ins and outs of the Elite One hearing. Apparently, it had been decided that he could race the rest of this season for Falco Roux, if he wished, and still maintain ownership of Accardi. He could have everything he wanted, everything he'd been working for...except the one thing he actually wanted.

Complicated emotions swirled within him, filling his chest and tightening his throat as he stared into the distance. None of it mattered, not without the woman he loved by his side.

Love.

He felt the realisation of how utterly stupid he'd been hit him, his stomach churning with nausea. All the houses in the world, all the world championship trophies and wins, all his businesses, all his success and money: none of it mattered without Astrid. He just hoped it wasn't too late for him to tell her that and fix what he'd broken.

London was awash with torrential rain and Astrid was infinitely glad that Jem had offered to take a very cranky Luca out to a museum for the afternoon so she could have some time alone.

She had managed to keep her tears at bay for practically the entire flight. Her heart had ached with loss and abandonment as she'd forced herself to recognise the fact that she had told Apollo she loved him, and it still hadn't enough. He wasn't prepared to put them first, the way she needed him to. It was done, and she felt broken once again, but she had survived worse. She had picked herself up before and she would do it again.

As she checked her emails, she spotted one that had been forwarded from Tristan and opened it, feeling her heart pump in her chest. Sure enough, it was the result of the Elite One hearing and, as her eyes scanned the lines of legalese, she felt a mixture of emotions.

Apollo could race again. Not only could he race again, he could also keep ownership of Accardi and still fulfil his contract with Falco Roux this season. He would travel the world as planned, and throw himself into his bid to become the next Elite One world champion, all the while having an entire racing team on his books too.

She closed her eyes. Well…that was that, then.

She watched the grey city day pass by through the window, and wondered how on earth she was going to survive this. Just then, she spotted an unfamiliar car parking outside…and a familiar tall figure running up to the house in the rain, banging heavily on her front door. She went to open it, shock filling her throat as a very wet Apollo stared back at her.

CHAPTER SEVENTEEN

'WHY ARE YOU HERE?' she asked over the roar of the wind and rain. 'You should be in Monaco right now, celebrating your victory at the hearing and planning for more.'

'I barely lasted five minutes after the news before I was hopping onto the jet to follow you here.'

'Why?' she asked again.

'Because I never should have let you go. Because it took me being offered every single damned thing that I thought I ever wanted before I realised that it would all be meaningless…without you,' he declared.

Astrid shook her head slowly, her heart beating frantically in her chest. 'Is this some kind of guilt trip? Because, if so, that's not fair. You knew that you had my blessing to stay and race. I just want you to do what makes you happy.'

Apollo stepped forward, gently taking her hands in his. He was freezing, and the wind and rain pounded down all around them, but she couldn't look away.

'*You* make me happy. With your bossy attitude and your big heart and your refusal to think the worst of me, even when I make the worst decisions.' He shook his head. 'I don't need to race or to own a team. I don't need any of it, Astrid.'

'But your vision, your plans...?'

He shook his head. 'The only plan I truly need is to follow whatever path keeps you and Luca by my side so we can make up for the years we spent apart.' He stepped even closer, the wind whipping his wool coat around them both as his eyes met hers. 'You said that I'm trying to have it all...but *you* are everything to me, Astrid. Everything. I should have told you that when I proposed. Or when I realised you were the woman I hadn't stopped thinking about for nearly eight damn years. Or even before that, on that fateful night in a lift in the dark, when our fates intertwined in the best way. I'm head over heels in love with you.'

Astrid felt her body tilt forward, reaching for him, needing to feel his strength surrounding her as tears spilled from her eyes and words completely failed her. Strong hands framed her face, wiping away the moisture but, frustratingly, he held her at a short distance.

'You're crying. I didn't mean to make you cry,' he said softly.

'What did you expect a girl to do when the man she loves makes a big romantic speech like that?' she sobbed, glorying in his low, husky laugh as she pulled him into a kiss. She was consumed with the wild need to reclaim him, as though they'd been apart for weeks rather than mere hours. When he pulled away far too soon, she fought the urge to complain, still reeling at the overwhelming riot of emotions that he had unleashed in her chest.

'I need you to understand that this isn't just pretty words and empty promises,' he said earnestly. 'This is me vowing never to walk away again. You were the first person to challenge me, to make me see how much my childhood affected me. How I chose to latch onto the limelight as a way of being in control, despite deep down craving something more stable. You showed me a version of myself that I never thought I could be: someone solid and dependable, someone real. It's only been a month, but I feel complete with you. Our time together in Grenada as a little family was true happiness. Being with you, having your trust and your heart…that's the only victory I want.'

A look of uncertainty crossed his handsome features. 'You told me that you loved me, my darling, and I froze like a coward. I want the chance to prove that I can deserve it if you choose to say those words to me again, and the chance to prove my own love for you. I want to prove it to you every single day for the rest of our lives.'

Astrid reached up, framing his strong, stubbled jawline in her hands. 'I love you, Apollo.' she said, letting the words sink in and glorying in how his eyes darkened with possession.

'You hurt me yesterday.' She met his gaze, knowing that, if he could bare his heart like this on her doorstep, she could do the same. 'I was heartbroken and furious, but I realise now that I don't want to give up on this: on you, on our future. Real love means giving each other room to make mistakes and grow past them. We found each other again after so many years, after so many obstacles in our way… I'm not going to give you up without a fight.'

'You really are made for me. My dream woman,' he murmured against her mouth, his body pressing hers up against the cool wood of her front door. 'My partner in life, my soul mate.'

'Your partner in jail if we don't take this inside and away from prying eyes quickly.' She laughed as he wrapped his coat around them both, ushering her inside and shielding their passionate reunion from the rain-soaked street.

They barely made it up to her bedroom before he claimed her with a wild abandon she'd never felt from him, leaving a trail of frantically removed clothing in their wake and filling her townhouse with the sound of their passion. As she rode towards her climax, she met his eyes and made her vow to love him and honour him so long as they both lived. He held her as they both fell apart, the beauty and connection of the moment almost too much to bear. And, once both their heartbeats had returned to normal, he whispered the same words against her skin.

He promised to love her, to honour her and cherish her as his, for ever.

Apollo felt the car shudder and shake as he rounded the final bend at the end of the track in the final race of the season. It was a tricky corner to navigate on soft tyres, and he had almost slid into the wall on the last lap. He focused his attention straight ahead, ignoring the chaos happening in his headset as his team mate cursed loudly.

Nina was five seconds behind him, holding off the lead driver of Accardi, who had been fighting it out with her for the past ten laps. She was a master at defending, her skill unmatched as she'd held off their competition and paved the way for Apollo to maintain his significant lead. This had been her first full season in a permanent seat and she was about to finish on the podium alongside him.

He focused on the track, holding his speed in check and praying his wheels held out as he guided the car onto the final straight. He felt every tiny lift, and the pull as he pushed his speed full-throttle, his body and the car seeming to meld into one as he held his breath and finally shot over the finish line.

Roars of triumph erupted in his headset from the engineers and team on the pit wall. He felt emotion clog his throat as he raised his fist high in the air above his head.

'Apollo Accardi, Elite One World Champion!' an announcer roared as the crowd's cheers became a wall of sound around him. Fuelled by pure adrenaline, it seemed like a lifetime before he could get the car off the track and park safely. Even longer while he ran at full speed towards the garage where he knew his wife and son had been watching every single lap.

'Papa!' Luca's small voice called out, loud and proud over the sound of the engines still finishing the race in the distance, and Apollo pulled off his helmet before lifting his boy high into his arms.

'You did it!' Luca cried, his little face filled with excitement in a way only a day at the track could cause. Apollo laughed, crushing his son into a tight hug and turning to greet his wife.

Astrid's eyes met his, watery with tears and pride as she too leaned in and joined the embrace with full force. 'You did it,' she murmured against his ear, the choked sound of her sobs like tiny earthquakes as her tears wet his cheeks.

'*We* did it,' he corrected her, closing his eyes tightly and releasing a long breath of pure relief.

They had finally done it. Against all odds, they had made it work as a team, with him travelling on the remaining Elite One schedule while Astrid held down the fort in their home in London and Luca absolutely smashed all his goals at school.

And, amidst all that chaos, they'd decided not to wait to get married. They'd eloped in Italy, on a sunny October afternoon, to a tiny chapel in Venice not far from where their story had first begun. His mother and Grayson had acted as their witnesses, with Jem guiding an excited Luca up to them so they could say their final vows together as a family. Izzy, Tristan and Nina had been the only other guests present, to keep the event intimate and calm. Once Luca had gone to bed, the grown-ups had enjoyed a welcome night of celebration before resuming the final stretch of the racing season.

It had been a hectic few months, and there had been moments of tears from all three of them, but overall they had learned how to prioritise one another and make it work. But, by God, he was ready to retire as a driver and switch his attention to cleaning up things at Accardi.

'My husband, the world champion,' Astrid said with a smile, leaning up on her tiptoes to place a fierce kiss against his mouth.

He was caked with sweat, and smelled like engine oil, but she didn't seem to mind too much as she deepened the kiss, much to the delight of the mechanics and the cheering crowd in the distance.

'I couldn't have done it without both of you,' he said, emotion turning his voice hoarse as he crushed them even tighter to his chest. All the trophies in the world could not amount to the pure treasure he held in his arms.

EPILOGUE

'I'M ALMOST ready, I swear,' Astrid lied, hurriedly dabbing a layer of powder high on her cheeks then staring at the selection of lip products she'd yet even to begin applying. She looked up, eyes landing on where Apollo now filled the doorway that separated her dressing room from their master bedroom. Mouth set in a firm line, Apollo cut an impressive figure in his designer wool coat and sleek white shirt, but the look in his eyes was one of fond impatience.

'You said five minutes. That was half an hour ago.' His tone was scolding, but his eyes were soft as he stalked across the room and slid one finger slowly along the thin strap of her midnight-blue dress.

'I know that look in your eye, Mr Accardi. And the answer is no.'

'No?' he repeated, brown eyes gleaming wickedly. 'It's like you want me to make us even more late today.'

'Apollo…' she scolded, his name turning into a groan as his lips lowered to her sensitive skin. His hands ran a sensual path along her shoulders and Astrid sighed as his fingers kneaded the delicate tension away, his thumbs working magic that he had learned and perfected in more than a decade of blissful marriage. Eleven years of bliss, to be precise…

She stared up at his reflection, taking in the handsome smattering of grey at his temples and the new designer beard that he was working for his latest sports-fashion crossover campaign with Falco Diamonds. Her husband was becoming a silver fox and she found him more attractive than ever.

Their eyes met in the reflection of the vanity mirror and he smiled devilishly as he clearly saw the undisguised heat in her own gaze.

'We haven't got time,' she breathed, gasping as his hands dipped beneath the neckline of her dress, brushing her nipple. 'Unless you can be fast.'

'Darling, you know how much I love a challenge.'

Then he lifted her, pressing her forward across the surface of her dressing table with absolutely no regard for the bottles of products he sent cascading down onto the carpeted floor.

'*Look* at you,' he rasped, sliding the silk of her dress up over her hips to reveal the rather risqué underwear she'd chosen. Strong fingers gripped the globe of her bottom, followed by a gentle yet possessive smack as he hummed in approval. He had just begun easing her dress up over her hips when a thundering of small footsteps intruded upon her consciousness, followed by the distinct sound of little-girl chatter heading straight for their bedroom door.

'How do they always know?' Apollo groaned in frustration, his forehead pressing between her shoulder blades. Astrid smirked, both of them collapsing into laughter as they moved to hide their state of undress with a speed that came from years of grabbing stolen kisses in various alcoves of their busy family home.

They had just enough time to right their clothing before their nine-year-old twin daughters came bursting into the room in a flurry of excitement.

'The car is waiting for us, Mummy!' Clara exclaimed with her usual vibrant excitement while her sister, Victoria, remained quiet, shrewd eyes taking in her parents' slightly frazzled appearances for a moment, before she joined in urging them to hurry so that they wouldn't be late.

It was the first day of the Elite One racing season. They still attended many races every year, as Apollo was still the owner of the now highly respected Accardi Autosport team, having rooted out the corrupt elements, including all three of his cousins. But this year they had a very new, slightly terrifying reason to be present at the opening ceremony.

'Are you ready?' Apollo asked, an equally nervous expression seeping into his usually calm features.

'Ready as I'll ever be, I suppose.' Astrid answered, placing her hand in his.

Apollo had stood in the garages of an Elite One Premio hundreds of times in his career, but today was different. Today it wasn't him standing in front of the monitors, performing his final checks, but his son. At just eighteen years old, the crisp maroon-and-gold suit of the Falco Roux team had yet to cling to his lean shoulders and wiry frame but, as predicted, Luca Lewis Accardi had grown into quite the handsome young man, standing a couple of inches taller than his father. He had not inherited Apollo's love for the camera, however, and his quiet, studious intensity had become his signature brand as he'd risen through the ranks of the Academy.

Astrid had given her baby boy one look and promptly burst into tears, necessitating Apollo ushering her away from the garage after a quick perfunctory hug and a choked whisper of good luck.

Luca didn't need luck; the boy was a natural in this high-intensity competition, just as he had been on the very first day Apollo had set him behind the wheel of a kart. His talent and drive for constant progress was infectious, so it had seemed a natural progression to everyone that Nina Roux would act as Luca's mentor once she eventually retired. Not just because Nina was also autistic, and understood the delicate balance that came with being a racing driver and having a neurodivergent brain but, according to Luca, because his father was much too performative and impulsive in his tactics.

Memories of how he had hated his own grandfather berating him and pushing him on the track was all Apollo had needed to give his son his blessing to drive for whatever team he wanted, whilst he watched from the sidelines.

Now here Luca was, performing his debut as an Elite One driver. The youngest driver ever to set foot on the track, he had already broken countless records, and the odds were he would continue to do so. Apollo could not have been more proud. Grayson Koh and Nina Roux stood alongside him as they waved the next generation of future champions off to the starting grid.

They walked together in pensive silence up to the corporate box, to watch with everyone else. Isabel appeared in the doorway, looking harassed.

'Thank goodness you're back; the children are running wild up here.'

'How many have you got now? Twenty?' Apollo asked, smirking when Grayson reached out to playfully punch him in the shoulder. Of course, he knew they had five, having officially adopted their third foster child to join their merry crew the previous Christmas. But it was fun to watch his old rival get steadily more outnumbered by the year. For all Apollo's previous jealousy, he and Grayson had become fast friends over the past decade, and they had both become equal partners in Apollo's enormously successful global campaign for equality in motor sport. He had even convinced Tristan to join them for a spicy calendar shoot, much to Nina's enjoyment.

The devilishly handsome owner of Falco Roux Racing appeared and greeted his wife, their five-year-old son Laurent hiding behind his legs. Nina would return to the garage to act as a consultant with her brother on the pit wall, but for now the six of them stood shoulder to shoulder as the teams took to the track and began warming up their tyres.

Apollo embraced his wife from behind, trying to take some of the nervous tension from her body with the heat of his own. 'Relax, *amore*. Luca's starting in pole position. He's going to win.'

'I know he will,' Astrid whispered, 'I just...wish he could win a little bit slower sometimes.'

Apollo laughed, turning her in his arms and placing a firm kiss on her lips. 'This is why you're not allowed in the garage.'

'I can think of one time in particular that you were very happy to have me all alone in the garage, husband.'

'I have no recollection of such a lewd act but, the minute this race is over, let's go straight down there and you can remind me.'

Astrid giggled and he leaned in, capturing the glorious sound with another deep kiss. He'd been so ready to take her earlier, he hadn't quite shaken his desire. It wasn't his fault that he'd married a walking seductress, determined to distract him with impure thoughts at every turn. She could have been wearing grease-covered overalls and he'd still have wanted her. Actually, that was another element he might add to their little role-play next time they wound up in an Elite One garage all by themselves…

The announcer's voice boomed through the speakers, cutting short a kiss that had already become too heated for public consumption, and Apollo laughed as his daughters teased them with loud kissing noises before turning back to continue playing and laughing with their friends.

Not just friends, he realised as he gazed around at their collective brood of happy offspring and the two other couples with whom they had shared their lives for the past decade. They'd become family to him too.

The thought buoyed him and he reached out to hold his wife's hand as they watched the cars line up on the grid.

* * * * *

If Driving the Billionaire Wild *swept you off your feet, then be sure to check out the previous instalments in The Fast Track Billionaires' Club trilogy,* The Bump in Their Forbidden Reunion *and* Fast-Track Fiancé*! And why not explore these other stories by Amanda Cinelli?*

Returning to Claim His Heir
Stolen in Her Wedding Gown
The Billionaire's Last-Minute Marriage
Pregnant in the Italian's Palazzo
A Ring to Claim Her Crown

Available now!